Deliver Us From Evil

True Cases of Haunted Houses
And Demonic Attacks

By J.F. Sawyer

Deliver Us From Evil

ISBN 978-1-9358568-7-0

OmniMedia Publishing LLC
Canary Islands, Spain

Book cover design and inside images by Ed Warren

www.edandlorrainewarren.com

Acknowledgements

The author and publisher wishes to express his appreciation for the collaboration of Ed and Lorraine Warren for their faith, guidance and aid in helping him to join the ranks of psychic investigators.

ORIGINAL PAINTINGS BY ED WARREN

For More information about Ed and Lorraine Warren, please check out the following:

www.edandlorrainewarren.com
www.seekersofthesupernatural.com
www.facebook.com/edandlorrainewarren
www.myspace.com/edandlorrainewarren
www.youtube.com/edandlorrainewarren
www.twitter.com/1stghosthunters

Table of Contents

Foreward

Almost everyone has experienced one form of supernatural activity or another, some have been driven to destruction by it. This book deals with investigations and reports of supernatural activities, such as the Demons that drove an 18-year old girl to practice human vampirism or the Ghost with mixed emotions that helped a Connecticut family renovate their home. Every story in this book is true, only the names of persons living or dead or places have been changed for obvious reasons. "Deliver Us From Evil" is a diary of some of the Warren's most spine tingling investigations.

Introduction

The supernatural - a vast area within which man's accepted knowledge and beliefs no longer hold true. It is a world of terrifying powers and nightmares; of voices from nowhere, footsteps in empty rooms; of demons and curses and apparitions; a world where fear reigns! But it can also be an area of gentleness and charm, of helpful entities attempting to aid those of the physical world.

Man is constantly seeking new frontiers for investigation, trying to learn all there is to know about life and the phenomena which influences it. There is a frontier which some courageous individuals have been studying since the beginning of time, although mankind as a whole has refused to - or has been afraid to - explore it, the region of the world beyond.

To date, only the most intrepid souls have dared to leave the light of the accepted universe to travel the dark pathways of the unknown. Man has always feared the unknown; but when that which was unknown is explained to him and becomes comprehensible, he learns to tolerate it and so no longer fear it. Make known the area of psychic phenomena to him, and he will no longer dread it. This, then, is the role of the psychic investigator. This is the task which Ed and

Lorraine Warren have set out to accomplish.

Although artists by profession, the Warrens have been seriously investigating the supernatural for over twenty-seven years, traveling throughout the United States and abroad, researching, and in recent years, lecturing on their discoveries.

Ed Warren's interest stems from his childhood in Bridgeport, Connecticut, where he lived with his family in a haunted home. His father, however, was a devout Catholic and refused, in spite of continuous paranormal occurrences suffered by every member of the household, to allow a belief in ghosts. In later years, Ed Warren began trying to prove that other people experienced the same phenomena that he, as a child, had witnessed.

Lorraine has naturally always been fascinated by psychic occurrences since she is a sensitive and has been having clairvoyant experiences all of her life. Although at first she was only slightly more sensitive that the majority of people (everyone is psychic and has the ability to develop his or her psychic powers to a greater degree) Lorraine's powers gradually grew stronger. The more supernatural happenings she experiences, the more her clairvoyance develops.

When Ed and Lorraine were first married, at eighteen, they used whatever money they earned from the sale of their paintings to travel to various haunted houses. They would sketch each house and learn all they could about its history, meanwhile trying to experience whatever it was possible for them to experience of the haunting. From the very first case, they kept a careful record of every investigation they conducted, so that they now have a few thousand thoroughly documented histories.

Until just a few years ago the Warrens' interest in the occult was known to only a few close friends. Then one day a collection of paintings Ed had done, about some of his more memorable cases, was seen by an art show promoter who asked Ed to exhibit them. Ed was at the show to answer any questions the visitors might have had about the supernatural. Since that time, the Warrens have been on the go constantly, investigating, lecturing, and doing radio and television shows. Members of the medical profession and even of the clergy are now contacting the Warrens for help in both human (ghostly) and inhuman (demonic) hauntings.

Of course, they have paid the price for their interest through many curses and strange accidents. No matter how serious the consequences, they feel that they have to keep on with their research and bring the results to the public. As the Warrens point out, the danger in dealing with psychic phenomena is in not knowing enough. It certainly is no field for amateurs. Their purpose in presenting their lecture programs is to interest more people in learning to become psychic researchers so that greater knowledge will eventually be brought forth.

Man is constantly seeking new frontiers for investigation, forever trying to learn all that he can about his earthly life; is it not also worthwhile for him to learn all that he can concerning his eternal life?

The stories which follow are all completely true cases. However, the names of persons living or dead have been changed for the protection of those involved, as have the names of buildings.

The Thoughts Of Ed Warren

The case histories that you will be reading about in this book concern mainly witchcraft and demonology. I realize that many readers will regard these subjects as sheer nonsense, remnants of the superstitious beliefs of times long past. Yet, there are those among you who are open minded enough to give serious thought to such ideas.

Men of science - doctors, physicists, biologists and even psychiatrists - could benefit greatly if they would look more closely into the field of parapsychology, especially if they would concern themselves not only with extra sensory perception and its relation to their fields, but also with the vast amounts of evidence of both human and demonic hauntings. I would like to refer these men to institutions such as Duke University, Georgetown University and Hospital, and St. Paul's University and Hospital, where they could learn of incredible cases of possession brought about by negative forces. In the case of one fourteen-year-old boy, the officials of the two hospitals and three universities mentioned above all verified that the boy was under the influence of amazing supernatural forces. Dr. J. B. Rhine of Duke University said it was the most fantastic case he had ever encountered in all the years of his investigations. The many doctors who examined the boy could find no logical reason, of any kind, for his behavior. In fact, the manifestations were of such a nature that no hospital or sanitarium would accept the boy during the time that the exorcism rites were being conducted. (This case has since been changed slightly and made into a very popular book and movie.)

Many people ask, "Why do you use mainly religious sponsored institutions such as Georgetown University and St. Paul's University for corroboration?" Where demonology is concerned, the answer is simple. Because they are religious organizations (in this case, Jesuit), they have great knowledge pertaining to the subject of demonology and how to deal with it. Of course, since all the great religions are deeply interested in the fight against the forces of demonology, those involved in working for these religions must necessarily be open-minded about a supernatural world. The evidence that they collect would be of great help in our work.

When the author of this book speaks of the performance of exorcism in some of these cases, please keep in mind that every religion, be it Catholicism, Judaism or Buddhism, has some form of exorcism rite in its doctrines. Exorcism is a series of ancient prayers used for the casting out of demons.

I was brought up as a Roman Catholic and, of course I believe in the teachings of Catholicism. I do not want to be misunderstood; I am not so narrow-minded to dismiss any other religion. I believe that any religion which teaches the love of our fellow man and the love of God is based on a sound foundation. Because I was brought up as a Catholic, I tend to use Catholic methods in my work. If I were in one of the deepest jungles of the world where so-called "primitive" witch doctors of a good nature were present, I would not hesitate for a moment to ask for their help in exorcism rites. Good comes in many forms and can be just as potent, just as helpful, in people we might regard as primitive and illiterate.

I believe that there are positive and negative supernatural forces that can and sometimes do manipulate our way of thinking and our way of life. I believe that even today, in our modern, scientific society, demons are just as much a threat as they were twenty centuries ago when a man called Jesus preached many warnings about them. If I am wrong in my beliefs, they can harm no one. If I am right and am taken seriously, I can help many.

At one high school where I lectured, they said that I frightened the students with my talk of these malign forces. My answer to this was, "Thank God. It only proves to me that they were really listening!"

As you read these pages, be logical in your thinking, but remain open-minded. I do not for one minute expect you to believe everything that is related to you in this book; I only ask you to think about it seriously while you are reading it and then ask yourself, "Is there a chance that these people may be right? If they are, what does it mean to me, personally?" I have seen atheists call on God, changing their way of thinking overnight when they've become involved with negative supernatural forces.

When one steps into the world of darkness, he had best go well prepared. A very wise man once said to me, "Ed, I would not go into some of the homes and communicate with the entities that you do for any price, especially where demonic forces are concerned!" Once you cross the threshold, you will be in great danger, as will be those whom you love. The negative forces against which you are working are clever, for they possess the cunning and knowledge of the ages. Those who have encountered these malevolent forces know this only too well. Ask a missionary priest or minister who has lived and worked in foreign lands if he believes in demonology and possession. I'm sure his answer will be most interesting. It is not that there are more cases of Satanism and black witchcraft in other countries. Actually, there are more cases right here in our own country. The difference is that we feel too civilized and scientific to even consider the possibility of demonic influences.

How many people are suffering the torments of Hell itself in some of our mental institutions today simply because psychiatrists have labeled them as paranoid schizophrenics when, in actuality, they may be under demonic possession?

Witchcraft, or Wicca as it once was called, is the oldest religion. It originated about 4000 years ago. The very word "witchcraft" conjures up many different kinds of impressions to those unfamiliar with its true meanings and with those who practice it. We are all too aware of the infamous witch trials of Salem, Massachusetts, and of the slaughter of thousands of innocent people in Europe condemned for so-called witchcraft practices during the middle ages. Even today, people found to be practicing witchcraft in some backward countries are persecuted for their beliefs. "Wicca" means "the knowledge of the wise." It refers to the knowledge for mixing potions and healing salves from leaves, roots, berries and the many other varieties of plant life. To the practitioners of this craft, Mother Earth is sacred, and they worship her.

They have learned to live with nature and know many of its secrets. Through a life of solitude, they practice psychic development; long hours of quiet meditation and concentration sharpen their extra senses. Precognition, the ability to see into the future, astral travel, out of the body experiences, telepathy, mental contact between living beings, and other aspects of the sixth sense are developed. Unfortunately, people with this type of knowledge are often considered by others to be strange and weird or even harmful. What we do not understand, or do not want to understand, frightens us. To be clairvoyant and to use this talent for the benefit of mankind can only mean progress, but our fear of this unknown world delays our progress.

At the same time, we must also consider what is commonly referred to as black witchcraft or devil worship. White witchcraft is used for the benefit of mankind; black witchcraft is used solely for the benefit of the black magicians, regardless of the consequences to others.

My own knowledge of both white and black witchcraft comes from my investigation of curses put on people, houses, and even certain locations, some of which you will be reading about in this book.

Some of the readers may be asking. "Can a curse really be placed on a person or object?" In answer, let me ask if you believe that someone or something can be blessed by a high spiritual person such as a priest, minister or rabbi? Through a blessing, vibrations of holiness and protection are placed on you. Now you may be asking, "Protection against what?" Against the negative or evil forces! In the Lord's Prayer, did you ever stop to really think about the words, "Deliver us from evil..."? What do they really mean? If a person of high spiritual caliber can place a blessing on you or your home, why can't a person with enough hate, calling upon the forces of darkness, place a curse on you?

Let me give an example of the effects of a curse placed on a certain object.

During my many years of investigation of satanic curses, I have met some very skeptical people. They usually respond with loud laughter to the suggestion that a curse can be placed on them. In fact, in the following case, a man actually died with a startled look of disbelief on his face when the ancient Egyptian curse in which he didn't believe was fulfilled.

The man was Britain's most famous Egyptologist, who had searched the sands of Egypt looking for the tomb of the god of medicine. He had been warned not to touch the statue of Osiris, the god of death, which would be found nearby. Professor Walter Amory was a scientist and he was not about to heed any such nonsense. Diggers at the site said that Professor Amory had many a good laugh about the curse and insisted on being the one to pick the statue up. The date was Friday, March 12, 1971. I wonder what the Professor was thinking about a few minutes after he had picked up the statue as his eyes rolled back into his head and he lapsed into a coma from which he never awakened. By the way, before Professor Amory left on the expedition, he had a thorough physical check-up that showed him to be in excellent health. Dr. William James of the British Museum was very distressed to receive the bad news of the Professor's death and remarked that it was most unfortunate how many archeologists met sudden death in similar cases!

People often ask me how I can prove that I am working with victims of real demonic possession. In some cases supernatural activity is visibly present, and yet in others I must rely on my experience with these elusive forces. My knowledge of demonology does not come from a university. There is no college course that can teach me the fantastic and incredible ways in which these negative forces of darkness work their malign deeds.

There are psychiatrists and psychologists who would

disagree with my findings in many of these cases. On the other hand, there are many who would agree. I have made mistakes in my work and no doubt will make many more, but I have also been right and have been able to help many of those who call on me. I will not turn my back on the victims of demonic forces simply because a skeptical public is not yet ready to accept the reality of the supernatural. It is strange that although many cases of modern-day demonology have been proven, skeptics still scoff simply because they do not want to admit, even to themselves, that there are things in both heaven and earth which just cannot yet be explained with a slide rule.

If you want the truth on these subjects, we will bring what knowledge we have of them to you. I think it is very important for the public to know exactly what the meaning of witchcraft and Satanism is today. Some of you, perhaps, are reading this book to gain knowledge, others out of curiosity, and yet others only to ridicule. Remember, by hiding our heads in the sand, we believe, like the ostrich, that because we cannot see our dangers they do not exist; we pretend that because it may be hard to see this supernatural world, the dangers of black witchcraft and Satanism do not exist. Unfortunately, they do exist.

When in this book J. F. Sawyer talks of the black mass and disgusting rites of Satanism, he is not trying to glorify them. He is trying to depict what is actually happening across the United States and throughout the world. How else can you become aware of many of these happenings unless someone like ourselves brings it to your attention? We can only do this through the pages of this book. Herein, you will find much of the information that I have acquired through my investigations.

The only way new truths can be discovered is through the study and exploration of these unknown subjects. However, I am not a witch and I am not a Satanist in disguise. I am solely an investigator of supernatural activity, witchcraft and demonology.

I believe that there is a God, and I wouldn't have it any other way. But how does one prove to others the existence of an invisible world, a world of fleeting shadows and malign entities? How does one prove that there is a world which is not of a tangible nature? We cannot see the wind, yet we know that it exists because we feel the sensation it causes. We can see its effects in the general motion of tree branches, grass and flowers as it silently moves along its course. In my case histories of both white and black witchcraft, I am constantly entering the invisible, intangible world. I am an explorer of the realm of darkness.

I am often asked to show proof. This I can do only through reliable witnesses, people who have gone through fantastic and sometimes terrible experiences. I cannot show scientific proof about a world that simply is not scientific. When we do come up with overwhelming evidence, however, skeptics shrug it off lightly, saying there is a logical explanation for the phenomenon. But, of course, they never come up with this logical explanation.

I know that there is a God and that He is called by many different names. Yet I cannot prove this scientifically. As I know that there is a God, I also know that there are demons which can obsess the thoughts and possess the bodies of humans. I have seen this! Skeptics say that these people are mentally ill; but does a mentally ill person talk in numerous languages that he has never heard, ridicule and attack a person holding a religious article, or even, as witnessed in many cases, actually rise off the ground?

The physical body of a person under demonic attack is almost constantly under brutal assault. Loud slaps can be heard and welts suddenly appear. The hair can many times be seen being torn from the head by invisible hands. The victim screams out in agony as inhuman laughter rings through the air! Meanwhile, the stench of rotting flesh or burning sulfur can permeate the area so badly that it causes nausea. Obscenities and foul language incessantly pour from the mouth of the unfortunate possessed victim, and his eyes are full of twisted hate and mocking derision. Does this sound like a person who is mentally ill?

When exorcism rites are performed, the person performing the exorcism is in great danger; he is the visible challenging the invisible. The exorcist must be of a high moral and spiritual nature. If he is a priest he must be a true priest in his every word, deed and action. The man who claims to be a true minister of God, and then in the same breath, says that he is only human and so indulges in practices unbefitting his office, will never be an exorcist. At least he should not try to be one. If he is weak and cannot resist human temptations, he will soon find out, to his great dismay, that the world of demons on which he gave so many sermons is all too real.

One need only go back into church records to find cases of true possession. Today as never before there is a need for ordained exorcists. The public is fascinated by witchcraft and satanic rites. We receive mail every week from people who have delved into the black arts and cannot control what they have summoned.

I have no quarrel with people who worship in whatever way they wish, but I do object to devil worship, to the defiling of graves, to the taking of human corpses to be used in ritual ceremonies, and to the stealing of religious articles from churches. "DO WHAT THOU WILT SHALT BE THE WHOLE OF THE LAW." This is their motto, and to this I wholeheartedly object.

I have been criticized by many people for talking on this subject. They say that I am inciting interest in witchcraft. But if these same people would bother to go into any neighborhood drug store and see the many books on witchcraft which are on their shelves, and realize the interest generated by these books, they would then know that I am here only to bring a warning to those who would involve themselves in the often dangerous black arts.

The Accursed Inn

Tucked away in a corner of Connecticut is a peaceful country village surrounded by rolling farmland. Not far outside of this village, on the old Boston to Hartford highway, stands the now dilapidated Stoneham Tavern, a 180 year old, sixteen-room former stage stop. While still an inn, the building saw its share of violence, as did many such pioneer taverns. Eventually it was converted into a private dwelling and was owned by three or four families before it was bought by Henry and Victoria D in the early 1900's.

Mr. and Mrs. D. and their family had many strange experiences in that house during the fifty years they lived there. The strangest and most heartbreaking event took place only a few years after they had moved in. Victoria had hitched up the carriage one morning to take her seven children to the one room schoolhouse about a mile down the road. But Laura, who was 14, said that she was sick and so was allowed to remain at home. Apparently she had the mumps. Victoria dropped the children off and returned to the house, only to find that Laura was missing! An intensive search was conducted by the family and by state police, but no clue was ever found - Laura had disappeared without a single trace!

In 1951, the house was bought by Charles and Florence V. They moved in on Good Friday and quickly began to try to restore the house to its original splendor.

One night a few months after they had moved in Florence and her twelve-year-old daughter, Sandra, were sitting in the kitchen reading. They were the only ones in the house. Slowly, they both became aware of someone walking about the empty second floor. As the footsteps began to get more frenzied, Sandra asked, "Who's that?" Florence, not wanting to frighten the child, answered, "It's probably just a squirrel." Just as she said that, there were two loud thumps, as if heavy objects were being dropped directly above them, and then silence. With that, Florence walked into her bedroom, also on the first floor, picked up a .22 revolver that she had for protection and, with it safely in her apron pocket, shakily re-entered the kitchen. Silence still. With a mutual sigh of relief, they both tried to go back to their reading. Upstairs, in a far corner of the house, an unknown presence again began pacing the floor, again began treading more heavily and loudly across the full length of the second floor, until, with a rapid scurrying of footsteps, the event again culminated in two loud thumps and then silence. Florence and her daughter quickly forgot about trying to read. Sandra was rushed off to bed, and, too frightened to go upstairs to see what caused the noises, Florence sat in bed herself and nervously waited for her husband to come home. Finally he arrived, and Florence jumped out of bed to quickly recount to him all that had taken place. Together they searched the house. There was nothing to be found. He told her that she would just have to get used to living in the country, there are all kinds of strange noises out there.

Still the footsteps continued. In fact almost everyone who ever stayed as an overnight guest left the next morning with some comment on the strange noises that they heard during the night. Florence's mother refused to stay in the house again after spending two nights listening to the unearthly footsteps pacing the second floor.

Florence's sister, Aura, who stayed overnight occasionally, complained of tapping on the outside of her second floor bedroom window, as if a tree branch were hitting it in the wind. There was not a tree anywhere near the window.

One morning she asked her sister, "Florence, who stayed in the corner room last night?"

"What do you mean? That room's always empty!"

"Well, I heard whispering and arguing all night long, but the only thing is, I couldn't understand what was being said."

Magic whispering is a phenomenon in many hauntings.

One very hot day in September of the year in which they had moved into the house, Florence was there alone, painting the walls of an upstairs bedroom. As she worked, the room slowly began to get colder, even though the sun continued to beat down just as intensely outside. The room kept getting colder and colder until Florence realized that she was shivering uncontrollably. Suddenly, even though she was looking out of the window, she knew that someone was in the room with her. She stiffened - this being was evil and hated her. Fear welled up in her. She was terrified, unable to turn around to see who was behind her. She tried to gather up her courage, tried to force her muscles to turn her around, when suddenly a freezing hand clamped down upon her shoulder! Trembling, not wanting to believe what she most feared, she slowly turned, the hand still on her shoulder. Then she began screaming over and over again as the ice-cold hand melted from her, for there was no one there! She yelled, "I don't know who you are or what you want, but you won't force me out of this house!"

Still screaming, she ran down the stairs, out onto the front porch and waited for her daughter to come home before she would go back in. She later told her daughter that she could get used to the walking, but what she experienced in that room was evil, terribly evil!

At certain times, usually while Florence was preparing dinner, there would be three loud knocks at the front door. Upon answering it, she would find no one there. Again the three knocks would sound, but before she could get to the door she would hear it open and slam shut, and someone very heavy would run right past her and up the stairs.

Keeping farm help became impossible. They were

terrified. One complained of an unseen person tucking him in at night! Another had the covers constantly pulled off of him. Then there was the incessant walking in the halls and around the beds to add to their misery.

Mr. and Mrs. V. had been living in the house for quite some time before something happened that was so frightening, she could never possibly forget. It occurred three times in one week and there was no doubt that it was meant only for her to experience.

Florence had gone to bed with her husband. The room was in complete darkness and she was on the verge of falling asleep when suddenly, she was jolted back to awareness. On the opposite wall there appeared a black mass, blacker than the surrounding darkness. Slowly, it began to glow, forming a ball. It started to grow; its color changed to pale yellow, to vivid orange and then to brilliant red. As it grew, it began to roar until it sounded like a blast furnace! Florence was petrified with fear as the roar became deafening and the brilliance blinding. She couldn't take any more. The fear, the noise, the blinding illumination of the entity was all too intense. She slipped into unconsciousness as her husband slept peacefully at her side.

Twice more that week Florence had the same experience. Each time she felt a greater, more powerful evil coming from the entity. Could it possibly be a warning?

In 1958, Sandra went away to college. That same year, Florence had another baby girl. Until that time, ghostly occurrences had somewhat subsided giving Mr. and Mrs. V. a respite. Their peace, however, was short-lived.

One cool fall night, Florence was in her living room watching television with one of the farmhands. The baby was asleep in her bedroom down the hall. Incredibly, a thundering roar shook the house coming from the direction of the child's room. Florence and the farmhand ran down the hall to the bedroom. The room was extremely cold although the house was very well heated. Once before Florence had felt that same freezing, damp cold, and remembered well the terror that came with it. Looking across the room, she saw that the other door, which had been latched from the inside, was swinging wide open. The thick, heavy latch was bent out of shape and torn from the wall. The radiator, which the door had hit when it opened, was still reverberating from the force of the crash. The farmhand then ran to the basement to see if the furnace had blown up. While he was gone, Florence suddenly had the distinct impression that this and most of the other happenings in this house centered around a young girl who was long since dead!

The furnace was working perfectly. No explanation could be found for the door having been forced open; that is, no earthly explanation. Nor could Florence's husband Charles, explain it when he arrived home. There is one more strange factor to take into consideration; both Florence and the hired hand heard the deafening explosion. The baby girl in bed next to the door that was smashed open, slept through it all unaware of what had just happened!

Neither this, nor the water faucets which were constantly being turned on throughout the house, nor the heavy furniture thrown about in locked unoccupied upstairs rooms, would force Florence to give up the house she loved so much.

She began to redecorate one of the rooms in the ell, stripping off layer after layer of old wallpaper, until she found beautiful, wide wood panels underneath.

She thought how nice the paneling would look until she noticed a large, splattered stain on one of the newly uncovered walls. She tried to wash it off, but it turned bright red, and then returned to the original dark brown color when it dried.

She believed that the stain was dried blood that had been there for years and was probably the basis behind the hauntings. This discovery caused Florence to trace back the history of the house. She discovered that about 200 years ago, two men had a fight over one of the serving girls that had worked at the inn. The two men killed each other in that room! Maybe they were the footsteps that Mrs. V. heard!

In 1962, after Florence and Charles had lived in the house for twelve years, they decided that they had had enough and they sold it. A number of tenants and owners have since come and gone but the occurrences continue.

Ed and Lorraine Warren were asked to visit the house by Mrs. V. and the present tenants. As Lorraine walked about the house, she began to feel as if there was a fire in the backyard. She could smell the smoke and feel the heat faintly as it began to drift around the side of the house. When she realized that what she sensed was not a fire that was currently burning, she asked if there had ever been a large fire in the past. No one knew. Then, looking out of a bedroom window, she envisioned the fields before the house was built. She saw a night illuminated by the many fires burning on the fields. In her vision she saw large stones surrounding each fire, and how each of the stones was scarred from the many burnings. Dancing around the fires were figures with their faces smeared with black sacrificial animal fat, obviously performing some sort of ceremonial magic. Next she saw, how those very same evil stones were used to later build the Stoneham Tavern. She then understood why the house was cursed. When Ed and Lorraine inspected the cellar, they saw the large, fire-scarred stones that made up the foundation.

Later during the evening Lorraine had another vision. A soldier came to the front door of the tavern. He signed in, and then sent his groom, a young orphan boy, out to stable his horse. In the barn, Lorraine could see a large black mass appear, and the boy just disappeared.

Lorraine next visited the room in which the door had

exploded open. Looking out a window, she saw herself as young Laura D. watching her brothers and sisters go off to school in a carriage. As she stared down the long straight road she felt the room becoming extremely cold. She turned, walked over to the fireplace and stood there trying to warm herself. The fireplace had been dismantled and sold a number of years earlier to a nearby historic association. Thus Lorraine had no way of knowing that there had ever been a fireplace in the room, but she was standing directly in front of where it had been. Suddenly she saw a huge black cloud forming in the corner of the room. Terrified, Laura ran into the closet to hide, never to be seen again. Just one more strange disappearance connected with the old Stoneham Tavern.

There are many other mysteries still connected with the old house, the evil still lurks there. Stoneham Tavern is again near ruins, and occupants come and go quickly as each experience his own brush with the macabre. It seems that the unearthly tenants of the old inn have added a new member to their eerie cast lately. In recent months the gentle, sad sobbing of a baby has also been heard wafting through the decaying corridors and rooms of the ancient house on the old Boston to Hartford stagecoach road. The spirits of the past refuse to give up their claims on the world of the present.

Possessed

Life is filled with a wealth of strange occurrences, many of which cannot be explained in "normal" terms. We can either make believe that such occurrences never happened, or we can accept them and look for their cause in the realm of the supernormal. The following is an account of one of those incidents for which the cause was found in the world of the supernatural, for this was a case of possession!

The story concerns two young cousins who, surprisingly, were total opposites. Anna, a shy, cute, soft-spoken girl, was very happily married and loved her husband and three children very much. Diane was a promiscuous, profane, vicious woman who was intensely jealous of Anna's happy life. Whereas Anna loved her children Diane, separated from her husband, hated all children, especially her own daughter, whom she often tormented terribly.

There is an old saying that as a man lives, so shall he die. On a bright, warm day in May, 1969, Diane, horrid in life, died a horrible death. The police called her death an accident; but there are those who believe, owing to the suspicious circumstances involved, that it was murder. Accident or murder, Diane's violent end was the beginning of a living nightmare for Anna.

One evening in July of 1969 Anna and her aunt, were using the Ouija board. It began as a typical sitting; the board gave no real answers to their questions. Then suddenly the pointer began moving quickly, spelling out a string of profanities and then, "Diane... Diane... murdered... I... was... murdered!" In startling succession followed reasons why, and names of those involved. Totally shaken, they put the board away for the night, and Anna went home. Thinking about what had happened, though, she became so intrigued with the idea of possibly communicating with her cousin's spirit that the next day she borrowed an Ouija board from her neighbor. In her home, alone except for her children, she began using the board for a few minutes each day. The answers to her questions at first meant nothing to her, but little by little more of what seemed to be Diane came through, throwing curses at Anna along with supposed information. As the contact with Diane's spirit increased, the time that Anna spent in trying to contact her also increased until she hastily rushed through her daily chores, anxious to get back to the Ouija. By this time, as she explained it, she had begun to feel as if she didn't belong to herself, as if something were making her use the Ouija constantly. She was right.

One night late in July, Anna awoke to the sound of heavy pieces of furniture being pushed about somewhere in the house. Her husband lay sound asleep next to her. She sat up, listening to the sounds for a moment, then got up and went from room to room, but the doors and windows were locked and nothing was out of place. She climbed back into bed, thinking that she must have been dreaming, and went to sleep again. The next morning, her compact was missing from her bureau. Infestation had begun!

Infestation is the beginning of a haunting. Sounds are heard and objects disappear. In this case, only Anna experienced any of this. She was to encounter much more.

Anna's sleep began to be filled with horrible dreams. In one which recurred, Anna was a spectator watching her body being controlled by Diane! She would fight to get her body back, but still she would hear her voice change to Diane's, see her own body become Diane in every way except appearance! Anna would always lose to Diane, no matter how hard she fought. And she would always wake up exhausted from these dreams, for the fighting that she did was real! Another recurrent theme in her nightmares was sex. She would dream sexually of things that she had never dreamed before, while her body would wildly enact them. She was frightened. It felt as if it wasn't her. She had never felt as sexy as that before! It was as if she were someone else! And her body! ...She just couldn't stop it!

The dreams continued, getting much worse. So did the

noises and disappearances. And so did the sex urges, for they were becoming uncontrollable even during the day.

One gloomy day late in the winter something slight went wrong for Anna. She went into a ten-minute tantrum, cursing at the top of her voice, using words that she had hardly even heard before, and had never used! A few days later, as her oldest child was sitting reading, Anna suddenly felt a tremendous hate for him and a desire to pick him up and smash him through the picture window. She forced the feeling to stop before she actually did anything. Anna's obsession was growing. Diane was beginning to come through.

Obsession is the next step in a possession case. First Anna had become obsessed with the Ouija board, followed later by an obsession with desires to harm her children. She experienced rage against the children and constantly swore at them and felt hatred for them. This behavior was unaccustomed for Anna and very appropriate for Diane. Feelings like wanting to rip open their stomachs and seeing their guts spill all over were finding their way into Anna's mind, and when they came, she was completely enveloped by them; she was prevented from doing what they commanded only by her own great love for her children, which so far had been strong enough to resist complete possession.

In these past few months, poor Anna had become enamored of her visions of death. In the middle of housework, she would abruptly stop to envision how lovely her children would look in their coffins, dressed so beautifully. She could see herself standing alongside of her children, smiling, feeling such great love for her dead children, and yet she would still feel hate for them and want to grab them and hurt them and tear at them! She thought, "How beautiful I would look in my coffin, dressed in my most enticing gown. My husband and all of my friends would look down at me and say, "Oh, how much we love you, Anna, and how attractive you are!" They would all miss me terribly."

Then Anna forgets about her housework and puts on a gown, thinking of her preparations for the grave, and dances her own mental Danse Macabre with her dead cousin, Diane.

Anna is in the throes of obsession and sometimes, possession. She is preoccupied with death and how she would dress for it (just like Diane, who was buried in her wedding gown). She is rapidly becoming Diane feeling promiscuous, very profane and vicious, hating and wanting to hurt her children. Soon, Diane will completely possess Anna. Diane, ever jealous of Anna in life, carried her jealousy with her to the grave. Earthbound by her violent end, yet desiring still her earthly life, what better way to come back than to take over her wonderful and weak cousin?

Unknown Visitor On A Winter's Night

It was Christmas night, 1971, in a southern Connecticut city and celebrations were in full swing. At one particular gathering, however, the party took a strange turn, which involved a twenty-two year old girl whom I shall call Julia. She was a beautiful and very sensitive artist, intelligent and sincere, who lived alone in a studio apartment. She was also an occasional student of the occult, whose interest was inherited from her clairvoyant mother. On this particular night Julia and her girlfriend were playing with the Ouija board trying to contact the spirit of the friend's father. Only statements that were garbled and meaningless came through. Using the Ouija in this manner though, allowed something else to come through, something that Julia would not discover until two weeks later. She would realize that the Ouija board must be taken seriously!

It was a bleak, icy, overcast Saturday night in January. Julia's boyfriend John left her apartment at 1 o'clock. They had spent most of the evening watching television programs on the occult and later discussing what they had seen. It was such a cold night that Julia decided to sleep on the sofa bed in the living room next to the heater. Except for the sound of the wind, her apartment was in silence.

Julia quickly fell asleep. In her dreams she heard John coming up the stairs to her apartment and opening the latch on the outside door. She called to him and told him that she was coming. Then she awoke! Strangely enough, she heard the sound again. It wasn't a dream at all! Someone was opening the latch to the outside door. Then the door itself crashed open. She thought it must have been the wind; perhaps she hadn't closed the door properly. Then every muscle in her body suddenly stiffened as she heard the creaking sound of the inside door opening. She thought that it must be a burglar. Then there was silence. Maybe it was only her imagination, or perhaps the house was creaking because of the cold night. Then she did hear a sound, faint at first but it kept getting louder, she could almost feel it coming closer. Something was on her bed! It touched her ankle ever so lightly and then touched her again, this time at the knee. It was crawling upward toward her head. What was it? Was it going to strangle Julia? The pressure increased, the whole weight of the creature was on top of her now, its hot breath in her face! Trembling, Julia opened her eyes and there, staring down at her were the great, slanted, yellow eyes of a huge black cat. Julia was terrified, she screamed at the top of her lungs. Very slowly, almost arrogantly, the cat turned and sauntered to the foot of the bed. Finally, with one last contemptuous look at Julia, it jumped off the bed and landed rather noisily on the wooden floor.

Julia sat up, her mouth open yet speechless, for at the foot of the bed, behind the cat, stood a girl. She was about fourteen years old and had long, straight blond hair, wearing what seemed to be a work shirt and faded blue denim jeans. Her cold, blue eyes stared at Julia. She began to walk toward her stiffly, militaristically around the bed, the cat at her feet, until she was only inches away from Julia. Her eyes seemed to hypnotize Julia in that open-mouthed position, keeping her from even the slightest movement. Then without a word, the ghost turned her back and silently glided out through the dining room, the cat in front of her, its tail arched to its back. Julia slammed her leg against the bed frame as she leaped out and ran immediately after the girl into the kitchen. There was no one there. The girl and the cat had simply vanished. She turned on the light and was suddenly struck by the realization that it had been so dark that she could hardly have seen her hand in front of her face, and yet she had seen both the cat and the girl in crystal clarity. The kitchen was empty, the doors and windows were all locked, and there was no sign at all of what had just occurred. Julia was puzzled but she was no longer frightened. She turned off the lights and went back to bed, trying to convince herself that those past few minutes were just a nightmare. She eventually fell back to sleep and awoke the next morning with only a bruise on her leg as a reminder of the previous night's experience.

(Ed Warren explains that Julia called in this entity on Christmas night when she and her friend toyed with the Ouija board. There have been many instances where someone has used the Ouija board and then suffered, sometimes quite terribly, at the hands of an unknown entity which he had summoned. On that Saturday in January, Julia had her mind on the occult all evening; this made her especially open and susceptible to an occurrence such as the one which happened.)

Julia soon dismissed this incident as a bad dream and would have eventually forgotten it if it were not for something else that happened to her, something so completely horrifying that it sent her running to get in touch with the Warrens for their help.

It was again a New England winter night, this time at the end of February. It was cold and dismal outside, but Julia's apartment was quite warm and cheery. Julia had invited her boyfriend John, her brother and her sister-in-law over for the evening. Her sister-in-law was to have a baby any day now. The girls thought that it would be fun to use the Ouija board that night to learn whether the new baby would be a boy or a girl. The Ouija refused to be serious and gave them garbled answers. They finally put it away and forgot it for the night. At about 11 o'clock Julia's brother and his wife left. John stayed and watched television until 1 o'clock. Once again, because it was such a cold night, Julia slept on the warm sofa bed in the living room. She awoke not long afterward feeling cold. Julia had never been cold like this before, it was a freezing, damp cold, almost as she imagined death would be! It seemed to be slipping over her slowly, covering her. It was the psychic cold which heralds the arrival of an entity from beyond. Suddenly the end of her bed dropped sharply as if an extremely heavy weight had fallen onto it. She jerked around toward it but was forced back flat against the bed when the weight smashed into her. It was crushing her, forcing her almost through the bed, making the bed's support bars, which she had never felt before, grind into her back. She was suffocating, gasping for breath, enveloped in a thick, airless black! Julia was panic-stricken. She was horrified! Her heart was pounding so hard she felt it would burst. She couldn't move a single muscle. She felt herself about to faint as icy hands stroked her jaw, caressed her cheeks and brushed across her lips. Suddenly, in that split second, she remembered something a friend had told her to do in cases such as this, and it gave her the strength to remain conscious. She tried to force herself to speak, but for the moment she couldn't. Her tongue seemed to stick to the roof of her mouth, her lips refused to move. Finally, as if she were caught by a giant whirlpool and being pulled down to her death, her lungs almost void of air, she managed to shriek out the words, "GOD BLESS YOU! GOD BLESS YOU!!" The weight recoiled from her violently, but it was still in the room. She could feel it lurking somewhere near her. She forced herself to overcome her fear by thinking of John. Julia thought as hard as she could about him, and then in her mind she could hear John's voice saying, "I love you, Julia, you are going to be alright!" She began to feel the warmth of love and happiness pass through her, and with that the malevolent presence departed, leaving Julia safe.

Calling for help had saved Julia from imminent danger of being destroyed mentally by the shock of the experience. Yet the entity itself was so totally demonic that even when she called out those words of blessing, it refused to leave. This made it necessary for a "spirit guide" to come forth and, as the Warrens explain, reassure Julia that she would be all right by using John's voice telepathically (a voice that she knew and loved and trusted). This gave her the confidence and stamina that she needed to overcome this malign being.

Unfortunately for Julia, it will take much more than that to completely rid her apartment of the haunting. Her unknown visitor has again come calling, and even now Julia occasionally awakens in the middle of the night to the sound of the door opening and the soft padding of a large cat strutting haughtily across the wooden living room floor.

Satan's Daughter

Two black candles flared on the dresser, their feeble light reflected in the mirror, creating a soft but thoroughly inadequate glow. Then, from out of the flickering darkness, a woman's voice arose, timidly at first but stronger with each word, chanting its ritual prayer:

"Hear me, oh ye who have the power to kindle the hearts of men. Fill him with love and desire. Hear me, oh Theriel, Ariel, Donquiel..."

In her sable gown and somber mourners veil, Lisa knelt in front of the improvised altar. Abruptly, the air around her became a thick, clammy cold, and, against her will, Lisa's gaze was forced up to the glass. Amazed and terrified, she realized that she was no longer alone! The hair on the nape of her neck rose as she started sobbing helplessly, for in the mirror Lisa saw not only her own reflection but that of a great, black mist with arm-like appendages looming over her, about to attack!

A year of terror, a year of near mental slavery followed before Lisa, then 18, was taken by a close friend of hers named Stan to talk to Ed and Lorraine Warren. The history of a demonic obsession and occasional possession unfolded before Lisa, right there, met again with her attacker.

Deliver Us From Evil

Why did it all start? As, unfortunately, in so many cases of this nature, it began with an urgent desire for something beyond the "victim's" reach; it began with a great need for the love of a particular man and a promise to do anything to get that love.

Lisa, who had been adopted when she was a young child by a wealthy New York family, found herself falling in love with a member of a motorcycle gang named John, who was her opposite in practically every way. She desperately tried everything that she could to make him notice her, but still he hardly seemed to.

While searching for a means of attracting his attention, she hit upon the idea of trying witchcraft. She didn't know then that it was actually a form of Satanism. She thought that it was nothing more than asking the gods of love for help. There was no connection between the two in her mind. If she had known then what she was soon to learn, she certainly would never have gone into it.

However, the ritual was performed, and during it that awful, malevolent being made the first of its many appearances. It comes so often now, just because of that one rite! He's not there all of the time, but he keeps coming a lot. Even when she doesn't see him, she can feel him - she can hear him talk to her and feel his touch. When the entity does come, she hears its voice softly whispering, telepathically:

"You are mine, Lisa, all mine! Remember your promise, Lisa? You said that you would do anything for me if I made John love you. Well, John does love you, Lisa, John does love you!"

Only after she had made John love her did Lisa realize what he was, but she found that she wasn't able to get rid of him - that the entity would not let her. Whenever she would try, the attacks would get much worse. She would find herself being forced to do things that she did not want to do. He makes her hurt those that she loves. He makes her shout at them and say things that she doesn't want to say. She cannot stop it - the words just keep coming out! He says that she can do anything bad that she wants to do, and he'll make sure no one finds out that she did it. He wants her to do these things! But she doesn't want to!

While sitting there talking to Ed Warren, Lisa felt the cold creeping over her again, and heard the voice hissing about her! She started crying hysterically, "Oh, he's here, he's here! Help me, please, help me!"

"What does it want?"

"He says that he's going to tear my heart out for talking to you and then he's going to put me into the sea of oblivion and never let me out! He says he's going to cut my tongue out!...

Ohhh... Please, please help me! I didn't know what I was doing! Now I'm worshipping Satan but I don't want to! Oh, no-o-o... he wants me to kill Stan! He's going to make me kill Stan! I won't be able to stop myself!..."

Ed finally forced the entity to leave. When Lisa had calmed down enough, to help her forget what she just went through, he asked her to talk about her life and interests in general. She began to talk about her love for writing, and then she remembered a story that she had written not long before, a story completely unlike any other she had ever written.

"It was about a girl who was alone in a pitch-dark room, waiting to meet her boyfriend, Stan. She kept calling his name over and over but he wouldn't answer. He still hadn't come. Then there was someone else in the room with her, and she knew it was Satan himself! She felt him smiling at her, staring at her. Then he said, "You are my daughter and you must do something for me. Remember your promise that you would do anything I asked if I made Stan love you? Well, the time has come, dear daughter. I want you to kill Stan!" Then the girl screamed, "No, I won't, and she began stabbing her demon-father with a letter opener that she had. All the while he just kept laughing. Finally, he was dead. But when she turned on the lights, she discovered that she had actually killed Stan!"

During each of the last few rituals which she had performed before she came to the Warrens (which she practiced even though she did not want to practice them), in the midst of the invocations she would hear her own voice echoing in the back of her mind saying,

"Hear me, for I am thine... Thy own humble servant, thy own daughter, Lisa..."

The next morning, having spent the night at the Warrens, Lisa and Stan left to go back to their college in upstate Connecticut. By this time, Lisa had realized that she must give up John and that she could fight the "demon" that was trying to possess her. But in the car on the way back, Lisa experienced a new phenomenon for the first time, a sharp pain across her chest which made it very difficult for her to breathe. The pain lasted for a few minutes before it abated. Twice more that day she felt the pain. It was completely unlike anything she had ever felt before. She was frightened. She thought perhaps she had a tumor or something else equally serious. That night the demon came to her again. She could feel the black cloud next to her bed, but she fought it away from her, kept it from getting to her.

The pain kept coming and going. A tremendous desire came with it, however; a desire to go back to Satanism and to kill Stan kept entering her, tempting her, almost winning.

But she fought it, and finally, after a few weeks, which seemed more like a few years, the demon began to leave her alone.

Everything seemed fine. School was going well, the attacks had ended, giving her the first peace she had known in over a year - her life was great. Then in English class each person was told to write a paper on a subject in which he or she was really involved. Lisa began to work on a paper about witchcraft and Satanism. The paper was due on a Monday, on the Friday night just before, Lisa had a strange dream in which the demon was trying to get back to her. That night it came to her again, after so many weeks of peace, and lurked about her room. She heard its voice calling her, telling her to come back. She forced it from her.

Saturday night she and Stan and a few others, her brother among them, were sitting in the campus cafeteria when the same intense pain that she had felt a few weeks earlier again crossed her chest.

"It was as if somebody were stepping on my chest, keeping my lungs from expanding," she said, "I could hardly breathe!" She then passed out, but with her eyes wide open, horrified. As the helpless onlookers watched, Lisa's body began to jump around wildly in the chair, pushing the table away and knocking various items off. She remembered nothing of the experience except what the witnesses told her; yet she did remember that as she was regaining consciousness, she heard loud drums beating and a piercing, ringing sound in her ears. Lisa woke up nauseous and had to be taken home to bed immediately. For the rest of the night, she was cold to the touch and terribly pale.

The next morning, Sunday, she thought that she was about to pass out again, so she asked to be taken to the emergency room at a nearby hospital. The doctor there said that her heart and everything else was fine. It was probably just a small seizure. He told her if it didn't happen again, not to worry about it. It could have been her nerves or anything. She wasn't satisfied with that answer, though. She wanted to make sure that it would not happen again.

Monday, Lisa went to the school infirmary. They sent her to a Hartford hospital for an electrocardiogram. She was given every sort of test imaginable to try to find a cause for her "seizure." The results of all the tests were normal. Nor could the cause have been a form of epilepsy, because her seizure had been of a totally different type. She was given a prescription for tranquilizers and again told that if the seizure did not recur, she shouldn't worry about it.

Thursday morning she awoke, again feeling sick. She realized also that her body was jumping about uncontrollably on the bed - the same kind of seizure, but this time she was conscious. She felt a terrible pain in her chest, and black spots were circling in front of her eyes.

As soon as she recovered, she destroyed all of her ritual items, making a strong effort never to be involved in Satanism again. Since then, the pains and attacks have again subsided, and once more Lisa knows comparative peace, although once in a while the strong desires still come to her, tempting her to go back to the fold, and tempting her to hurt Stan in whatever way she can. At those times, if she is with Stan, she forces herself to walk away without saying a word, fighting those desires with all of her strength. Sometimes, too, she wakes up in the middle of the night and again feels the demon in the room with her. But seldom does she hear its voice any more. She has finally regained the control of herself that she lost so long ago. It would seem that Lisa is slipping from the grasp of the demon.

Stan, however, is still afraid of retribution from the demon, for it was he who insisted that Lisa go to the Warrens for help. It was he, in effect, who took Lisa from the reaches of the entity.

Strangely enough, Stan has recently begun having terrible nightmares in which he hears a voice demanding that he stab his parents to death. In these dreams, he fights a losing battle and finally does kill his mother and father with a sharp kitchen knife. These dreams, especially after all he has gone through with Lisa, are particularly frightening to him. But even more frightening - he has begun to have those urgent desires to murder, those persistent, tempting, hard to resist desires to kill, even while awake. Is it just his overactive imagination? Or is it to start all over again?

Demon In The House

The demon that you will read about in the next few pages chose a small and usually quiet town not far from Boston. Its shaded, tree-lined streets and silent, friendly houses bear mute witness to the normal tranquility of the village. Except for a rash of suicides centering around Maple Street in the past years, this tranquility has seldom been broken.

John and Joyce S. live on Maple Street, they moved into their home in 1965. If they had known then that the mysterious events which began happening soon after they arrived were just a prelude of things to come, they would have moved right back out again. Their home became the center of an unbelievable nightmare for in it, ever malicious and harmful, resides an inhuman entity... a demon.

On a beautiful sunlit afternoon, shortly after they moved in, they had their first experience with the supernatural. While sitting at the kitchen table, sipping coffee and talking over plans for their new house, a lamp, which was fastened to a wall, just seemed to tear itself loose, screws and all, and fell to the floor about six feet from where they sat. For the next couple of months, almost every time someone sat at the table, the same thing happened. John and Joyce were baffled.

One of the chairs at the table had belonged to Joyce's grandmother and although she didn't believe in witches and witchcraft, she thought just maybe there could be a connection between her dead grandmother, the chair and the flying lamp. The entity played along. When she had the chair burned, the lamp stopped falling.

Joyce was relieved that the confusing episode had finally come to an end and she quickly tried to put it out of her mind. The demon was not to be denied though. A few weeks later Joyce was once again confronted with the unknown.

One morning while sitting at the kitchen table, she felt compelled to turn around and look at the wall behind her. She saw a triangular shaped light, about two and a half feet in height, and appearing on the wall with it, the name - Gregory Carter-Smith. She was no longer aware of anything except that light and a voice she seemed to hear inside her head. She asked the voice what it was doing in her house. The voice answered, "I've lived here for thirty-five years!" She then asked the voice if it liked her. It answered, "In my heart I do, not your husband, only you." The entity, who for the time being had taken the name of Gregory, was getting bolder!

From that moment on it seemed that John and Joyce were never totally alone in the house. When John was not there, Joyce would hear whispering behind her. When she turned around, it would still be behind her. The magic whispering was always mumbled, it could never be understood. One summer every night at precisely 11 o'clock they heard someone running down the back stairs, but no one was ever seen!

 www.edandlorrainewarren.com

It was late one particularly dark night and Joyce had just fallen asleep. John was in bed next to her just about to drop off to sleep when he heard something that caused him to look up. There, just off to one side, he saw a floating, burning bright orange ball of fire! It was the size of a basketball with two slanted slots where eyes should have been. He was frozen with fear! He wanted to reach out to his wife, but he couldn't move. John knew it had to be some kind of demon. As it moved closer it seemed to sap all of his strength and willpower. It passed over him and moved to the other side of the room and as it did, he felt that he was about to die. With the realization of his probable death came his last surge of strength. John used this new power to concentrate, to reason and to fight a mental battle with this malevolent demon. As he fought his will increased until finally, with the greatest of effort, he won and the fireball faded away. John held his wife in his arms for the rest of the night. In the morning he told her about the demon he had faced the previous night.

A few months later John and Joyce had their second child, they named him Dennis. Their first child, Theresa, so far hadn't been bothered by any of the supernatural occurrences. With Dennis, things were to be different.

In the middle of winter on a frozen, cheerless night, John and Joyce experienced their next encounter with the unknown. They had just gone to bed when they heard a loud explosion and saw a blinding flash of light just outside their bedroom window. Joyce jumped out of bed and ran over to look out. She noticed that the window was open at the top about an inch . . . yet the window was still locked! When they searched the house, they found that the windows in the living room and in Dennis' room were in the same condition. It was almost as if the windows had shrunk.

Time passed and more and more of the mysterious happenings seemed to surround Dennis. Many times, in the evening after Dennis had been put to bed, John and Joyce would hear the sounds of banging and jumping around or crying accompanied by the high pitched voice of a woman. When they reached his bedroom they would find him staring blankly out the window, shaking with fear and perspiring profusely. When he was questioned he couldn't answer coherently, and never remembered the next morning what had happened to him the night before.

Joyce's sister-in-law, Betty, babysat for her one night and she, too, heard the woman's voice upstairs, this time it seemed to be arguing with Dennis. Each time she went upstairs to investigate, the voice would stop. Betty's restlessness caused the family dog, whose name was Lady, to become restless too, so she let her out. Betty tried to settle back to her reading. Suddenly she heard a man's voice behind her say, "Hey, Lady!" When she turned around, no one was there. Betty didn't know whether the voice was addressing her or the dog, but she knew she had heard the demon!

Joyce's most frightening meeting with the demon occurred, once again, just after she had gone to bed one night. She could feel the covers being pulled from her, and there from the very place where she lay, the apparition of a woman arose! She stood up and framed by the moonlight shining through the window, Joyce could see her in crystal clarity dressed in a housecoat, the moon reflecting on her long brown hair. She tried to cry out to John, but fear had taken her voice. She watched the woman walk out of the room, and a moment later she heard Dennis scream. By the time she got to Dennis' room, the woman had gone. Joyce knew that she had seen the woman whose voice had tormented her for so long; she would never forget her!

During the times that they weren't being plagued by the demon, John and Joyce tried to lead normal lives. Their encounters with him seemed much more frequent.

While John was cleaning out the attic, he felt someone grab onto his ankles and pull his legs out from under him. This caused him to lose his balance and he was easily pushed out the window. Fortunately for him, he managed to hang onto the inside casing and climb back inside. The attic window was about thirty-five feet above the ground. A few weeks later Dennis had a similar experience. Luckily John was there to catch him.

On another occasion Joyce's mother agreed to babysit for her. She had heard about the strange voices in the house and hoped that she could hear them for herself. As the evening wore on she began to relax. The family dog, Lady slept at her feet. Suddenly she heard what seemed to be a low, menacing growl. It was as if a mad dog was in the room, right behind her! Lady didn't move; she was sound asleep. Joyce's mother knew it couldn't have been Lady that made that sound. As if she was defying the demon, she shouted at it that she was not afraid, she told it to get out and leave her alone! She was not bothered by the demon again that night.

John and Joyce continue to notice many more "little" things. Not too long ago they noticed the banister seemed to sway back and forth when they walked down the stairs. They have both seen the fireball again. It even seems that they have become ill more often and have more little accidents around the house. Joyce said that twice unseen fingers tried to choke her. She is terrified of the house and refuses to be left alone in it.

In the spring of 1972, Joyce heard the woman's voice again coming from Dennis' room. In an attempt to reach the room while the woman was still there, she rushed up the stairs without calling for John. The woman was gone, but Dennis was lying there, his arms outstretched, as if reaching for someone to pick him up. He seemed to be in shock staring blankly, shaking and perspiring profusely. Joyce ran to the head of the stairs and called to John for help. When they returned to the bedroom, they noticed a depression on the mattress as if someone was sitting next to Dennis.

John and Joyce decided that the only way to fight the demon

was through prayer. Being Catholic they bought a crucifix for each bedroom. When they had finished hanging the cross on the wall in Dennis' room, he began to jump up and down and twist about, trembling and sobbing as if he were in agonizing pain. Suddenly the cross jumped from the wall and fell to the floor. Three times it was hung up, three times it flew from the wall and landed on the floor. The fourth time John nailed it securely to the wall, this time the demon gave in . . . for now!

At times it seemed that Dennis was possessed. Many times he had knowledge of deaths that occurred many years ago, deaths of people even John and Joyce had not known. What could they do? Would the demon ever leave their home?

John and Joyce considered many explanations for the events happening to them and their family. They even looked into their past for the answer. Before they had moved into this house, Joyce had made extensive use of the Ouija board. Could that be the cause of their encounters with the demon? Whatever the cause, the heartbreak they suffered was not about to end. Their house is haunted by a demon. How long it has existed in that house is unknown, but John and Joyce hope that it will end soon. Lately, intense psychic cold spots have been coming and going in various places in the house, and a huge black mass has been seen several times lurking in the corners of the bedrooms. It seems as if the demon is telling them that what they have seen up to now is only the beginning, their misery has just begun!

You See, He Put A Curse On You

Ruth is an attractive 20 year old who, since her divorce has lived with her parents. She had lived a fairly simple life consisting mainly of taking care of her young daughter and doing her part of the household chores. Her life changed recently because of a chain of unexplained, incomprehensible events. Ruth had never believed in the supernatural but soon had more proof of it than she could ever hope for. Ruth had believed, at first, that it was her parent's house that was haunted. She soon had horrifying proof that it was not the house it was she.

Furious clouds tumbled endlessly overhead while thunder exploded amidst great bolts of lightening. The earsplitting din of the storm made that night in March 1972, even more dreadful, and Ruth's baby daughter Linda, found it difficult to sleep. Sometime after midnight Linda cried for her mother to take her downstairs to the bathroom. Stumbling through the thick darkness, they made it down and back again without major mishap but something made Ruth uneasy. She almost convinced herself though, that the storm had given her the strange feeling. After she had tucked Linda safely in bed, she bent over to kiss her. Linda was staring, wide-eyed, right past her mother. Ruth suddenly froze. She felt a tingling, warm substance numbing her feet, then her legs, oozing higher and higher. It felt like thousands of tiny fingers scratching, pushing, prodding her back, her sides and squeezing against her. This groping mass slipped further around Ruth, almost enveloping her, it reached over her shoulders and caressed her cheeks. She managed to turn around in the hopes of seeing who, or what, was trying to suffocate her. There was a single brilliant flash of lightening . . . and then, nothing. The room was now as empty as it had been earlier that night. Ruth ran from the room, it was dawn before her mother could calm her down.

With the slow, painful passing of each day, the event repeated itself. Not only did she encounter the entity at night but also, now she experienced its presence in broad daylight. She soon noticed that each attack was preceded by about five minutes of warning sounds - whispering and tapping. She still could not do anything to stop the attacks but at least she knew when they were coming and she could try to be with someone. The entity would glide up behind her and eventually tower over her, threatening to engulf her. Although its dimensions were never exactly the same, she could feel that it was much taller and wider than she. It was shaped like a small cloud. She felt that the entity was male, an incredibly evil male. She knew that if she ever allowed it to completely surround her, something terrible would happen to her, perhaps she would even die.

It soon became almost unbearable. She feared going to bed at night, she feared getting up in the morning. Ruth became desperate; her mind was in turmoil. In an effort to protect her sanity she went to a psychiatrist for help.

The psychiatrist wasn't much help. He told Ruth that the events that she described just couldn't have happened to her. He said that she had an over-active imagination and once she realized that, these things would stop happening to her. She left his office with a prescription for tranquilizers, in the hopes that they would calm her down and allow her to take control of her mind again.

That night she took even more than the recommended dosage. She did go to sleep, but not for long. Soon she felt the all too familiar cloud once again overtaking her, surrounding her body. The pills didn't work.

Ruth was now deeply worried, what could she do? She didn't really believe in the supernatural but she thought if it was, just by chance, perhaps she could overpower it with the help of religion. Ruth hadn't been going to church lately, since her divorce. She was a Catholic though, so she simply went to the Catholic Church nearest her house. She asked the priest to listen to her story. She told him of the entity, how it seemed to come from behind her and almost envelope her. She spoke of her visit to the psychiatrist and his recommendation of the pills. She said that she might be possessed by the devil and only a religious blessing would send him away. The priest wanted no part of this kind of talk and told Ruth to go home, take the pills and stop acting like a child. Ruth was not satisfied so she went to another church, hoping that she might receive a blessing there. The Monsignor seemed very friendly to her, he listened closely to everything that she said. He told her that she had experienced a "light exorcism". He blessed her, said that it would never happen again and sent her on her way. He told her that any time that she wanted to talk to him, he would be there.

That night the entity came again. The blessing that she had received from the Monsignor had not helped, but Ruth felt that she would like to talk with him once again. When she returned to the church, the Monsignor was not there but she was allowed to talk with another priest of the parish. She felt that this priest treated her in the same way the first priest treated her. He told her there was nothing wrong with her, he thought perhaps a few trips to a psychiatrist would help. He said the reason she was experiencing these things was that she had a guilty conscience. She felt guilty because she hadn't been attending church lately, and she knew this was wrong. He told her that if she would start going to mass again, her problem would soon go away. Ruth just couldn't accept that advice.

The attacks on her continued, each time Ruth believed that the entity would suffocate her and she would die. She thought that the only solution for her would be to leave that house. She packed her belongings and she and her little daughter moved in with her sister-in-law. The entity attacked again.

It was then she realized that she was doomed, somehow she had become involved with the supernatural, it was after her.

Why was this happening to her? What had she done in her life to warrant this? She began to look back on her life, trying to determine exactly when these encounters with this thing began. Then she saw it, a connection that was so contrary to all her beliefs that even then, after all she had experienced, she found it hard to accept.

Early in March, Ruth had been asked to go out on a date by a man whom she really didn't know very well. She did know, however, that what she had heard about him, she didn't like. She had heard that he practiced Satanism. She didn't believe in the occult, but it was enough to make her wonder about his reputation. When Ruth refused to accept his invitation, he went into an unbelievable rage. In fact, he threatened her and told her that she wouldn't be sleeping at night any more. Ruth couldn't believe that anyone could get that excited at a refusal of a date. That was the last time she heard from him, she erased the incident from her mind.

Almost as if to confirm her suspicions, the day after Ruth had made the shaky connection between that man and the attacks on her, a woman who lived in the apartment downstairs, came up to see her. She told her that she had been told of Ruth's misery and wanted to help her. She said that she had known the man and he had, indeed, put a curse on her. The woman said that the only way that Ruth could lift the spell was to perform some counter-magic. She suggested that they go to a cemetery and cast the counter-spell. Ruth thanked the woman for her concern, but said that she did not think that she cared to use something that she did not believe in . . . the supernatural.

She almost reconsidered the woman's offer after the entity struck again, this time endangering her sister as well.

Ruth was driving home one night; her sister was in the car with her, when she heard those strange whispering sounds again warning her. She forced herself to concentrate on the road, praying that her concentration would not allow the entity to take hold of her. In spite of her effort the warm, numbing feeling began making its way over her back, running its unearthly fingers through her hair. It began edging around her sides, crawling over her waist, making it more difficult for her to drive. Her fingers were becoming numb, she could hardly hold onto the wheel. Her foot was becoming heavier, weighing down the gas pedal. The car began racing faster and faster swerving wildly over the road. Ruth's sister could not see the entity but she could see, in Ruth's eyes, that something horrible was happening to her. She drew her breath and began to scream and at the same time reached over and held down the horn. The entity could not fight Ruth's intense concentration, the screaming of her sister, the blowing of the horn and it retreated to its murky world of nowhere.

Ruth was now at the point where she could not go out in public, she had to have a person at her side at all times. She could not be left alone or she would be attacked. It was at this point that she contacted Ed and Lorraine Warren. Their investigation revealed that a spell had, indeed, been cast on Ruth. As time passed, it strengthened its hold on her. Was it too late to help Ruth? Ed and Lorraine decided to send her to an exorcist whom they felt could help her. After spending many days learning the exorcism rites, Ruth came away with the first feeling of peace she had known in weeks.

Her feelings of contentment were short-lived, though. The attacks came back with even greater force. Attack after attack came upon her with incredible intensity. Hysterical, frustrated beyond endurance, Ruth began to feel that every hope had deserted her. She began to consider that last despairing act.

One last hope remained for Ruth. The Warrens knew a high spiritual yogi who offered his help on Ruth's behalf. He had her come and stay with him so that he could offer protection to her whenever an attack came. After violent fights with the entity, the attacks diminished. As of this writing, Ruth has spent much time totally free of her demonic entity. The curse has been turned back, hopefully, to its sender.

To Dwell With A Devil

Tangled black oaks frame the ancient, dingy white farmhouse. Its windows seem to be staring back at you, inviting you to enter. The inside can best be described as turn of the century. Drab, faded religious pictures hang where they have hung for years. Starched white doilies which have undergone thousands of washings and careful ironings, now sit on the arms of colorless overstuffed chairs. From the outside the house is deceptive, its many angles give the impression that the house has many rooms, yet it has only seven. The sagging, wood frame, dwelling houses memories of many generations. The present generation consists of sixteen-year-old Kathy, her mother Irene, her father Fred and her sister Pat. Her older brother died by drowning in 1970.

The haunting was first discovered on a cool fall morning. When Irene awoke that morning she discovered that the fringe on her bedspread had been tightly braided during the night. Pairs of stockings and slip straps had also been braided. Irene was upset to think that someone had come into her room while she was sleeping. Why would anyone do such a silly thing? The braiding happened again the next night, then again each night for about a week. Irene couldn't stand it any longer so she cut the fringe off the bedspread.

That night Irene awoke from a sound sleep with the uneasy feeling that there was someone else in the room. She felt someone lift the covers and climb in bed with her. It was a young girl. As the girl's body moved closer to her a biting, piercing cold turned Irene to ice. She reached for the light hanging on the wall just above her head. As she did, she could feel the girl slip out of bed. By the time she had turned on the light, the room was empty and the girl had disappeared.

For days afterward rooms, which were known to be empty, echoed with the sound of pacing feet on wooden floors. Doors were heard opening and closing even though no visible person was there. All members of the family heard these eerie sounds. None wanted to believe it!

Not long before he died, Kathy's brother had witnessed the terror hidden in the house. One night he was awakened by the terrible feeling that he was being crushed. When he opened his eyes, he could make out what seemed to be a man lying on top of him, smothering him. Just as he was about to cry out for help, the man rose from the bed and walked into infinity.

For Kathy the haunting had just begun. She was alone one

evening, in the living room, reading. Slowly, she became aware that she had been hearing, in the back of her mind, a voice calling to her from somewhere else in the house. It was almost muffled as it called out her name. She began to listen for the voice now . . . it seemed to be coming from the cellar. Her heart began pounding wildly. Kathy was not a particularly brave girl but, for some reason, got up and headed for the cellar door.

Kathy's trembling hand reached for the doorknob. She forced it to grasp the handle. Almost automatically it turned slightly and the door opened.

A child's voice could be heard teasingly calling Kathy's name. She wanted to run out of the house and call for someone to join her in the search of the cellar. Something forced her to the basement. The voice could be heard very clearly now, it seemed to be right next to her. She groped in the dark for the light, touched the cord and pulled it on. The room was flooded with light; there was no one there.

Kathy never seemed the same after that experience. The entity began to obsess her and she became the victim of almost nightly horrors.

A few nights later a strange uneasiness came over Kathy and woke her. Still half asleep, she glanced quickly around the room as if to assure herself that all is well. When her eyes came upon her sister's bed, she saw the answer to her uneasiness. A tall erect figure, pure white in color and holding a trident, stood next to Pat's bed. As she watched, a host of vague, white apparitions entered through every conceivable opening in the room, each bearing a great knife. The hordes continuously advanced on the bed, making repeated attempts to attack her still sleeping sister. The great white spirit guide stood guard over the girl, fended them off and sent them back to where they came from. Kathy watched the silent ghostly battle, too stunned to cry for help, too weak to run away. Moments later she slipped into unconsciousness and slept until morning.

As the weeks went by, all of the family heard the nightly crashes of heavy objects downstairs. Investigation revealed that nothing was ever out of its place or broken. All were unnerved by the sounds of whispering voices that carried up from the cellar, faintly echoing throughout the rooms in the dead of night.

Kathy soon found strange thoughts entering her mind, thoughts of despair and destruction and even suicide. She felt that she was the cause of the unearthly occurrences. She must be punished! Over and over again, the voices in her mind told her that she was evil. One night she couldn't resist the compelling urge, and she was drawn into her bedroom for penance. Once alone, she took a large metal cross and began heating it with a lighter. When the crucifix had absorbed as much heat as it could from the flaming lighter, she pressed it against her upper arm, branding her skin and burning it deep into the flesh. Four times more she repeated this until her upper arm was a mass of hanging flesh. The entity was gaining its hold of Kathy, her punishment was finished - for now. She was losing control, and she didn't know how to stop it.

Kathy's desire to punish herself was foremost in her mind. She knew that her entity was responsible for this torture. She decided that the only way she could rid herself of this evil was by suicide! The malign spirit could not have been happier - that was precisely what it wanted her to do. She locked herself in her room and prepared to set it on fire. She felt that the fire would destroy the evil with her. At the moment she struck the match her sister knocked on the door. The suicide was put off, for now at least. The entity lost a minor battle, but there were more to come.

Disturbances continued. On her way to bed one night, Kathy found herself following a woman with a long white veil up the stairs. As the woman neared the top of the stairs, she just faded away!

Later that night Kathy was awakened by the sound of a light switch being snapped on and off. Although she could hear the switch, the lights did not go on or off. This too, happened night after night. The entity had found yet another way to torment Kathy. Once again she felt that she must punish herself for being evil, this time the sharp blade of a razor resulted in her hospitalization.

Alone in the silence of her hospital room Kathy heard voices. They sounded like the droning chants of many nuns and monks who she felt surrounded her. They kept telling her to go home where she belonged.

When Kathy returned home she continued to be driven by the entity. Apparently it was no longer satisfied with having her harm only herself. Kathy now felt the need to do physical harm to others. The world was evil and the people in it must be punished. At that point Ed and Lorraine Warren were called in to investigate.

Lorraine could feel an entity in the house, particularly in one of the upstairs bedrooms. This one seemed evil, as if it were lying in wait. There were other vibrations in the house, almost as if more than one unearthly inhabitant lived there. She could feel the childish, playful spirit that Kathy could hear whispering and calling her name. The upstairs demon was the one that utterly took possession of Kathy's mind.

Kathy still remains seized by obsession. The family's nights are filled with whispering voices and apparitions continue to walk the stairs and lurk in the rooms of the old farmhouse.

The Voodoo Doll

Mrs. C. bought another doll for her rather large collection. The doll was quite interesting. It was about a foot tall and had a cute white cloth dress, little shoes, long hair and a face made strangely frightening by brightly painted lips and cheeks and staring eyes that seemed almost too real. Tied tightly around its neck was a noose - the doll had been hanged.

Mr. and Mrs. C. owned and operated a rest home; they lived on the grounds. Mrs. C., who was the doll collector, placed the "witch doll" in a wooden box when she returned home with it. She said it was just a precaution, after all it was supposed to be cursed. She was not a superstitious woman, but it was best not to take any chances.

A few days later, after deciding there's no fun collecting if you can't show it off, she took the doll from the wooden box and moved it to the glass display cabinet where she kept her collection. The cabinet was always kept locked because many of the dolls were quite valuable. The only key was in the constant possession of her husband. In spite of this, by the next day the witch doll had disappeared. A thorough search was made of the house and the rest home, the doll could not be found. Finally, because Mrs. C. had looked everywhere else, she searched her bedroom. There, in the bureau drawer,

Deliver Us From Evil

she found her witch doll. Many times since then her little witch doll has, for no apparent reason, run for the cover of her bureau drawer.

Mrs. C. loved to buy dolls at auctions. She felt that each doll had the secrets of its previous owner somehow within it. The doll that she bought in Jacksonville, Florida was one such doll. This one turned out to be a voodoo doll!

From the moment that she bought the doll, her peaceful life became just a pleasant memory. From that moment on, her life entered another dimension.

Even those who knew nothing of the doll's history felt a strange uneasiness when they saw it. They felt almost as if the doll were watching them. Many said that the doll was evil and they refused to even touch it. Mrs. C. decided to put it under a glass dome hoping that this would help to hold in what she thought might be evil vibrations.

When one of the elderly patients at the rest home saw it encased in its glass dome, he said that he got the eerie feeling that it was trying to get out, but it just couldn't. He said that it gave him the willies.

Mrs. C. decided, one day that she was being foolish. That doll could not possibly be evil or harmful. After all, it is only a doll! She took it from under the glass and placed it on a table for display. Then her problems began.

The Voodoo Doll

At the time, a one hundred thousand dollar addition to the rest home was being constructed. Work was progressing on schedule and completion was not far away. Less than one hour after the doll was removed from its glass dome, state inspectors discovered that the contractor had made a series of mistakes which forced officials to change the home's status from that of rest home to convalescent home. A costly, unfortunate change! Incredible other complications arose which began to be resolved only after the doll had been given to Ed and Lorraine Warren.

Mr. and Mrs. C. had a son who had always been a healthy child. Shortly after Mrs. C. had purchased the voodoo doll, the boy began to complain about feeling weak. Doctors could find no apparent reason for his condition. One of New England's leading pediatricians ran extensive laboratory tests on him, but could find no cause for his malady. His condition worsened. Doctors could prescribe no medication for him. There was no diagnosis. He became so weak that doctors gave up all hope; it was just a matter of time. It was for this reason the Warrens were called in. Lorraine could feel evil vibrations coming from the voodoo doll and advised that it be removed from the house. Once it was removed, the boy began to recover. To the doctor's amazement, in a few days, he was completely recovered.

During the three years that Mrs. C. owned the dolls, she suffered spells of great depression. She did not realize that there could be any connection between the dolls and her mental suffering. Soon, Mrs. C. noticed that every time she spent any length of time near the collection she would suffer violent headaches. She decided that she would destroy the dolls and bring an end to their evil magic. The dolls meant a great deal to her, she had collected them from many parts of the country. She finally gathered enough courage to do what she really didn't want to do and picked up the voodoo doll to throw it in the fire. As she did, she could feel what seemed like hatred and sickness coming from the doll, flowing into her body through her hand. She quickly threw it on the floor. A minute later, after she told herself that it couldn't have happened, she picked up the doll to try once more to destroy it. Once again she was prevented from doing so. She returned it to the shelf. She was later to discover that dolls such as hers cannot be destroyed without first performing certain rites over them. Ed Warren later explained, "The reason that the dolls are in existence now is that they failed to work when they were supposed to. If they had worked on their intended victims, the dolls would have immediately been destroyed, releasing the forces stored in them by the magician.

The witch doll with the noose around its neck was designed

to make the victim hang himself. The voodoo doll, which has real hair and fingernails and taken from the victim, was probably meant to be hung in a rainspout or similar area at the victim's house so that as it rotted away, the victim would too.

The fact that neither doll was destroyed means that the curses did not work but reverted back to the magician, destroying him. His spirit would then have been trapped in the doll, to be released only when the doll was finally destroyed.

If certain rites are not performed over them, then the person who destroys the dolls would become the next victim of the curses."

When the Warrens took possession of the two dolls, they put them on display in their museum in the basement, under glass domes. They had circumambulism performed around the cases by a high spiritual person. Circumambulism is a series of prayers said in a circle formed around the objects, to hold the vibrations in.

One night a retired Navy commander and his wife came to visit Ed and Lorraine. The wife became intrigued by the dolls and asked if she could pick them up. Ed, of course, would not let her and explained why. All evening the woman's attention was drawn back to the dolls. When Ed had left the room for a moment the commander's wife went to the display and picked up one of the dolls. The circle of protection was broken. She gasped, dropped the doll and she said it had burned her. She did not bother with the dolls for the rest of the evening. The damage was done.

The commander and his wife left later that night for their home in another town and Ed and Lorraine went to bed.

At about 2:30 in the morning they were awakened by the sound of loud crashing and banging. It was coming from the direction of the basement. Ed raced down the stairs. When he reached the museum he saw all of his paintings and artifacts piled in the center of the room. The two dolls, still in their places, were lying on their sides. The room was filled with the stench of burning sulphur. Ed opened the basement windows to air it out. In order to protect the dolls he took them out to his studio which was in a separate building.

About forty minutes later, Lorraine was again awakened. This time the blinking of the studio lights shining through her bedroom window woke her. She woke Ed. He went to the window and saw nothing. He told Lorraine that her imagination was causing her to see things. They went back to bed. A few minutes later they were back on their feet again when, this time, they both saw the frenzied flashing of the studio lights. When Ed searched the studio, he found nothing.

While the commander and his wife were on their way home from their visit that night they suffered an accident that almost took their lives. The road was perfectly clear, visibility was excellent and there was not a car in sight. The commander had pulled onto one of the main highways near his home when, out of nowhere, blinding headlights reflected in his mirror and, in a split second, there was a tremendous crash. Their car was pushed over seventy-five feet down the road. The windows were smashed by the impact. The seat belts, which were strapped around the commander and his wife, were snapped. There had been absolutely nothing on the highway when the commander pulled out, yet seconds later he was struck from behind. Neither driver had seen the other car. No one had been drinking.

Four people almost died that night. Was it because the circle of protection had been broken from around the witch doll and the voodoo doll? It is impossible to be sure. Consider this statement made by the commander to the police shortly after the accident and later to the Warrens:

"I looked up into the mirror and saw those blinding headlights and noticed that they formed sort of a halo and . . . God, I swear that in the center of that halo were those two dolls, staring at me, laughing!"

Haunting In New Haven

New Haven, Connecticut, architecturally, combines the very modern with the classic settings of the old town and Yale University. Outside the center of the city are countless narrow streets lined with hundred-year-old wooden houses, now all converted into two or three family dwellings. The yards around these houses usually consist of a five-foot wide strip of grass on two sides, a driveway on the third and, in back, a small rectangle of dirt with a carriage house, now serving as a garage. It is in precisely this type of house that our next case begins.

It was a two-family home, stairs led up to the third floor but the rooms were not finished. When the Stillman family bought the house, they knew nothing of its history. They were quickly told by the neighbors that the man who had lived there before them had hung himself in the attic - and the rope was still there, tied to the rafters!

One night soon after they had moved into the house, Ann Stillman felt a strong fear of putting her bedroom light out and going to sleep. After several minutes she convinced herself that she was being childish and she reached over to flip the switch when she felt something very cold touch her arm. It touched her again, and before she could withdraw her arm, an unseen hand took hold of her wrist. Ann struggled to release herself from the icy grip. When she had freed herself, she noticed what appeared to be welts on her wrist. Upon close inspection, they seemed to form letters creating a word in a language she was not able to decipher.

Many times Ann's husband, Stanley would come home from work and find the lights on all over the house. At first this did not bother him. Soon he heard doors opening and closing and footsteps on the second floor, even when he knew there was no one else in the house. Stanley did not know exactly what was causing the strange events, but he did try to avoid being alone in the house any more.

Ann and her daughter Debbie, traced back the history of the former tenants and discovered that all of the men who had ever lived in the house, no matter how kind and gentle they were before they moved in, became very cruel and violent after they had moved in. They also seemed to become prone to unusual accidents. Another unusual fact that they uncovered, all of the previous owners lost the house, usually through mortgage foreclosure. In fact, the man who had hung himself in the attic did so because his mortgage on the house was being foreclosed.

Wedding bells soon rang for Debbie and she and her husband moved into the vacant apartment on the second floor. As in her father's case, when she was alone in the house, she would hear noises like the opening and closing of doors and the sound of footsteps in the unused attic. Debbie became used to the sounds. She even began to refer to the sounds as coming from her friend, the ghost.

Debbie's husband, true to tradition, soon became extremely violent. He would shout and scream at Debbie for no apparent reason. Once he threw a lamp at the wall, it crashed into a hundred pieces. She became terrified of him. Occasionally, when she came home from work late at night, she would find that her husband had taken all of the bulbs from the lights on the stairs leading up to her apartment. She often had the feeling that her husband, in a violent mood, would be hiding on the stairs waiting to strangle her. Whenever the lights were out, therefore, she would ask her friend the ghost for help. Without fail, Debbie would feel a cold hand take her by the elbow and gently guide her up the stairs; she knew at those times that nothing could harm her. Her guide was never seen but was always there to help her.

Debbie's father came home one night and again the lights were on in his downstairs apartment, he knew no one was home. He went to a pay phone and called Debbie and asked her if she would, with the aid of her friendly ghost, go in there with him. At first, with the exception of the lights being on, everything seemed to be in order. When they entered the living room, Debbie saw a man sitting on the sofa. He was very tall and looked to be about forty years old. He smiled at Debbie as though they had been long time friends. Thinking that the man was a friend of her father's, she looked toward him for an introduction. She could see that her father could not see the man. She looked back at the man just in time to see him vanish.

The Stillman's remodeled the attic and Debbie moved up there. Debbie's sister Sophie and her family moved into the second floor apartment. She had heard of some of the strange things that happened in the house but she refused to believe any of it. Besides, no ghost could frighten her!

One evening Debbie and her sister exchanged words over some minor disagreement. In her anger she wished that her ghostly friend would come and pull Sophie out of bed. That night, Sophie had hardly put out the light when something had grabbed her by the ankles and pulled her to the floor. She had a very difficult time explaining to her husband what she was doing on the floor.

Sophie had a son who was of high school age; his name was Bob. He decided to have a party one night and invited his girl and a few other couples over. Although they had all heard stories about the "haunted house", none of them believed them. Shortly after they arrived they began poking fun at Bob and his haunted house. They taunted him to bring out his ghost. In a joking mood, they turned out the lights to see what would happen. Almost immediately a small ball of light appeared and began moving around the room, leaving a trail of smoke. The lights were quickly turned on again and the sphere disappeared. The room was searched for some evidence of trickery, none could be found. The group built up their courage with false joviality; once more they turned out the lights. This time the boy who had mocked the presence of a ghost in the house most vehemently, suddenly found himself on the floor. No one was near him at the time. The group decided that they had tempted the unknown enough that night. They went on with their party, they needed no more proof.

Bob often awakened in the morning and found himself on the floor. He could remember having strange dreams on those nights and thought that he had fallen out of bed as a result of them. One night he just couldn't fall asleep. Soon he heard the footsteps that he had heard many times in that house. Bob listened as the footsteps came closer. (His room was separated from the hall by only a bamboo curtain.) He heard the footsteps stop. He realized that there was someone standing behind the curtain, he could see him silhouetted against the dim hall light. He pretended to be asleep, keeping watch out of a slightly open eye. As if he were being punished for spying on the ghost, he found himself on the floor, this time the bed was on top of him.

A few days later Bob came home from school very tired. So tired that he decided to take a nap before dinner. He lay on his bed with his arms behind his head, when suddenly he felt the room beginning to spin. He thought this meant that he was going to faint, so he decided to sit up. He couldn't sit up - he couldn't move! He tried to shout for help, he couldn't speak! Soon, he began to see people, people that he had never seen before, all standing around him, staring at him. Then, just as quickly as it started, he stopped spinning. The people disappeared, and he could hear the sound of chuckling, the ghost had once again showed that he is the master of this house in New Haven.

The hauntings continue in the house. Several weeks ago Sophie thought she heard a noise in her bedroom. It came from under the bed; perhaps it was a mouse. Bob went in as his mother quickly exited. He searched, but to no avail. Then, just as he was about to get off his hands and knees, after looking under the bed, he saw, standing in a corner a tall, beautiful woman dressed all in black, staring at him. He felt a cool breeze in the room. The woman was there all right; he had no doubt of that. Yet, after about ten seconds, she just disappeared!

Doors still slam shut by themselves in that house in New Haven, footsteps are still heard in the empty rooms and apparitions are still seen. The author learned, just before publication of this book, that the Stillman's are in the process of losing the house through foreclosure, as did so many of its previous owners.

So many people that have lived in that house have known intense sadness, misery and heartbreak. The building is like a sponge, it soaks up the emotions of all who have lived there. For as long as it stands it will remain an abode of melancholy and a house of horror.

The Incredible Case Of Maria

Maria had to have help. Her life, since she was a child was filled with evil. Her mind and body had been taken prisoner by demons. Ed and Lorraine Warren were her only chance. Maria told them of her mother's death through a voodoo curse. She told of her unmarried daughter getting pregnant, her other daughter getting hit by a car and almost dying in the hospital. Even her sister was touched by her possession when she broke her hip and had to be taken to the hospital.

Maria came from a poor Italian family. When she was seven years old a man named Angelo became interested in her. Her mother, old-fashioned in her ways, considered Maria fortunate to have someone with a good job interested in her. She did all she could to make her look older, she even allowed her to use make-up. When Angelo would come to visit he would ask Maria to sit next to him and offer her fifty cents to stay and talk to him. To a child fifty cents was a large sum of money, but she always refused. Quite often, on Sundays, Angelo would take Maria out for a ride or a picnic. Her mother would always force her to go.

Maria did not like Angelo touching her, pawing her. She prayed for help to defend against his constant attentions.

One Sunday when she was eight years old, she walked into the kitchen and didn't see Angelo. Her mother scolded her for ignoring him, and made her apologize. Angelo sat there staring hungrily at Maria as if she were a beautiful young woman instead of a child. In order to get to her bedroom she had to walk right past him, so she skirted around him in a large circle, thus avoiding contact with him. Again her mother shouted at her and scolded her for being impolite. Angelo had come to take Maria to a nearby amusement park. She begged to be allowed to stay home. Her mother insisted that she go with him. Once more she prayed for help to resist him.

Angelo tried to make Maria enjoy herself. He took her on many of the rides, bought her ice cream and hot dogs, but Maria was miserable. Then he made her walk with him into a big field near the park. There was no one in sight, the grass was quite tall and Maria was afraid. Angelo bent over to kiss her and at the same time threw her to the ground. Maria screamed and, suddenly, an older man and woman appeared out of nowhere. Angelo seemed terrified. He helped Maria off the ground and took her home. Maria or her family has not seen or heard from Angelo since.

When Maria was nearly nine, she and her family moved to another house in the same town. She was very cute, a bit chubby, was light-skinned and had auburn hair. Within a short time she began to change drastically. Her eyes, which had been bright and sparkling, became dull and sunken. Her hair turned dark and her skin became sallow. She lost a great deal of weight. Her family became terrified. Doctors could not explain it. Her mother bought a skin bleaching cream to try to lighten her skin. It seemed to be a total physical change, almost as if she changed into someone else!

At about the same time Maria's uncle Peter came to the United States from Sicily and moved right in with the family. He became very fond of Maria and insisted on calling her "Rose" because that was his mother's name.

One day, Maria and some of her friends were out playing when it began to rain. Maria was quite wet by the time she got home, so she went directly to her room to change. Just as she had taken her wet clothes off, Peter walked in the room. He walked over to her, put his arms around her and covered her with kisses. Peter tried, from then on, to get close to her and be alone with her whenever he could. Many times she had to tell him that if he did not leave her alone she would tell her mother.

The older she became, the more tightly controlled her life became. She wasn't even allowed to go out with her girl friends for fear that she would meet another man. Peter was tremendously jealous. Maria was not allowed to go anywhere unless it was with him or her mother. Maria's mother would beat her with a strap if she even said "hello" to another boy.

In order to help support the family, when Maria became eighteen she was allowed to work. She found a job as a sales clerk in a store. One of the other sales clerks that worked with her felt sorry for her and introduced her to a male customer. Maria and her new friend knew that if her mother found out, they would both be in trouble. He seemed so nice and the only times they could see each other was at lunch, so Maria could see no harm in having lunch with him.

A few days later her new friend, whose name was Roy, asked her to go out with him that night. In order to get her mother's permission, the other sales girl told her that she needed Maria's help at her home that night. Reluctantly, Maria was allowed to go.

Maria really enjoyed herself that night. They had all sat around and talked, but she really felt free. When she saw that it was almost ten o'clock, she began to get nervous and asked Roy to take her home. He drove her there but when they got near the house, they saw Peter and her father standing there, under a streetlight, waiting for her. Roy drove past the house. Maria quickly got out, ran up the driveway and climbed the outside stairs to the second floor. There, on the landing stood Maria's mother with a basket of firewood which she proceeded to throw at Maria, piece by piece.

Maria was too bruised to go to work the next day. When Roy learned this, he went to her brother's house and asked him to arrange a meeting with her family. Reluctantly, they met with Roy and, oddly enough, they liked him. They even encouraged her to go out on dates with him. As a matter of fact, Peter even advised her to marry Roy.

Ed and Lorraine were puzzled by this. Could it be that Peter was clairvoyant and knew that they would never be happy together? Further investigation revealed much information about Peter.

Peter was somewhat well known as a healer. He would take those who were ill or who had broken bones upstairs to the attic, where he would perform various rituals over them. When they left, their ills would be healed. He spent many nights reading, into the early morning hours, from a book that he would show to no one. On the days after he had performed his rituals, there were always traces of blood to be found on the floor. Those are not the ways of a true healer, they are the ways of a Satanist!

Arrangements were made by the family for Maria to marry Roy. She didn't really want to marry him, not now at least. Invitations had already been sent out and her mother said that she would disgrace the family if she didn't marry him. She finally agreed.

Maria and Roy had been married for about three years when Peter decided to return to his wife in Sicily. Not too long after his return, he died. Maria, although not what would be considered happily married, was nonetheless happier than she had been before her marriage. Even that was to change. After Peter's death, Maria's troubles really began!

Roy bought Maria an Ouija board. She thought that by

using it she could find some of the answers to the family problems that were plaguing her. They played with it together at first, but soon the board demanded to talk with Maria alone. At first she "talked" with the board only in the evening. Soon she spent more and more of her time with the board until it became an obsession with her. Her troubles seemed to multiply with her increased use of the board.

One of the problems which prompted Maria to buy the board was her mother's failing health. She soon discovered that her sister-in-law, who had never liked Maria's mother gave her what she called an amulet to wear over her heart for good luck. One day when she was very sick, she showed it to Maria and asked her if it could have anything to do with her sickness. Maria took the cloth bag from around her neck and ripped it open. There, inside packed in sawdust were thirteen rusted coffin nails. The damage was done, however. Not long afterwards Maria's mother died of an enlarged heart.

Maria's use of the Ouija board became more intense and a somewhat macabre love affair blossomed. The board told her that it loved her! It described itself as a man, forty-five years old with light eyes, skin and hair and had grown up in Rome and had known Maria in a previous life. (How strange, his description so closely resembled Peter.)

Maria asked him if he was a God-loving man. He answered in the affirmative and recited passages from the Bible, as if to prove it to her. He even called her Rose which was Peter's nickname for her.

The more that Maria used the Ouija board, the more strange things happened throughout the house. They heard footsteps in empty rooms and on the stairs. Doors and windows opened and closed by themselves. There always seemed to be someone else in the room.

The Ouija still insisted that it loved Maria and would ask her to kiss the board each night before she went to bed. When Roy felt in an amorous mood and made husbandly advances toward her, a loud slap would be heard and his head would be jarred to one side. The invisible entity was extremely jealous of Maria. If she let her thoughts wander to other men, she would feel the slap!

Maria soon fell in love with the entity that came through the Ouija. She had to "talk" with it as often as possible. Many nights she would be awakened to the soft whispering of a voice calling, "Maria, Maria," or sometimes, "Rose, Rose." The board was calling her to talk with it.

As time passed Maria began to worry about her love affair with the board. She even began to doubt the validity of the entity. She turned to the Bible and prayed as often as she could.

One night while reading from the Bible, she felt the familiar urge to make love to the Ouija. She tried to force the desire from her mind. She pleaded to be left alone. The board would not listen. Maria finally gave in. The planchette began moving wildly, it told of the entity's previous life. It promised to come back in a new body, meet Maria and marry her. It spoke of Maria's mother being there with her relatives and how happy they are.

Maria was still angry with the board for interrupting her reading of the Bible. She told the entity that she didn't think that he was a "soul of God". He became angry with her. He told her that her mother was angry also. He told her that she had spoiled it for him. The master was angry with him and would not let him return again to talk with her. No sooner had the Ouija board "spoken" those words the room became saturated with the smell of human excrement. Deodorants and cologne had no affect on the odor. Finally it faded away.

For the first time Maria realized the evil that the board had produced. She took it to the backyard and poured gasoline on it in an attempt to burn it, but it would not burn. Maria became hysterical, she smashed the board against the stonewall in her yard. When it was splintered, she poured gasoline on it again, this time it became engulfed in flames. As it burned, Maria felt as if her whole body were on fire. For three days and three nights, she felt as if she were standing in the oven of Hell. Her skin turned brilliant red. She wanted so desperately to pray for help, but every time she tried to pray, her body would become paralyzed. Her skin began to tighten over her body. The veins in her body became visible;

they almost burst through her skin. She was in excruciating pain. She begged for relief, but no mortal could help her.

After those three days and three nights of horror Maria began to be visited by another entity. This time it was a woman who had an incredibly evil chuckle. One night she saw the woman.

Her nephew Brian was on leave from the Navy and chose to visit Maria. One night both he and Maria's daughter went out on separate dates. Maria always left the hall light on; the last one in would shut it off. This way Maria could tell at a glance if all were safely home. On this particular night, she heard the key in the lock signifying that one of the children was returning. She heard the door open and shut and heard the footsteps on the stairs. There, on the stairs, she saw a girl with short brown curly hair coming toward her. This girl was not her daughter. As Maria watched, the girl just seemed to disappear!

A few minutes later Brian arrived home. Maria decided to check to see if she could have been mistaken. Her daughter was not in her room. She knocked on Brian's door and then entered. Her daughter was not in Brian's room either. A few minutes after Maria had returned to bed she heard knocking on the kitchen door. Upon investigation she found that her daughter was just returning from her date and had forgotten her key.

Maria felt that there were now two entities haunting her. She decided to seek help from her church. She explained her problem to her priest and asked him to bless her house. His blessing had no affect on the entities. In fact, each time she sought help, the frequency of the attacks on her seemed to increase.

A friend of Maria's told her of Ed and Lorraine's ability to help and begged her to go and see them. After learning all the facts in the case Ed and Lorraine decided to consult a deep-trance medium in the hopes of learning the secrets of the other world harassing Maria. The medium had never met her.

An informal circle was formed in the living room of Maria's house. The medium asked her for an object that related to the hauntings. By the use of psychometry she could pick up vibrations and make contact. Maria gave her a letter that she had received from Peter through automatic writing. The medium withdrew into her trance, holding the letter in her hands. The entranced medium spoke, this time in a deep masculine voice:

"I want to cry. Lord, I want to cry like I've never cried in my life before. If I could take this letter I would crush it because it is my whole life. I have poured into these lines not only my words but also my whole soul, all that I am. Everything that I could possibly be is in there. I am not evil. Do you understand? I am me!"

Ed Warren interrupted the voice that seemed to be Peter and asked if he practiced witchcraft in life.

"No, that is not the word we use. When I was alive, I became aware of a certain power that I had. I knew that it didn't come from God. Therefore, I attributed it to he who is the brother of darkness. Because I wanted to control Maria so much, I begged and entreated and used that power. I did not realize that it carries over after death!"

Maria then asked where the blood that was found on the attic floor came from. Before Peter's voice could answer another voice, this one slow and guttural tried to force its voice through the entranced medium. Then Peter's voice:

"Haven't I betrayed enough mysteries to you? Aren't you repulsed enough? Do you have to know more?"

Maria said that she had to know everything. How and where he died. She said that if he sincerely wanted to help her, he would tell all.

A long period of silence followed. It was evident that there was more than one entity trying to use the medium. She was in deep concentration, her eyes were completely closed, her head was bowed. Then a new voice came:

"I would like to help you, Maria."

Ed Warren picked up the conversation with this new entity. "Who are you?"

"Diablo."

"What are you doing here tonight?"

"You called me!"

"There are many devils, what is your real name?"

"Satan!"

"Are you among those who attack this woman?"

"No."

"Then why are you here tonight?"

"It's an open invitation. Anyone can come."

"What is the real reason? Do you have something to say?"

"I care. I want very much to help. I am so sad. I have been sad for a long time. I don't want to do this any more! I don't want to be here any more! God, I ask you to relieve me . . . relieve me!"

"Do you believe in God?"

"Yes."

"You cannot call upon him?"

"Is there a way?"

Then the sound of mumbling as if all was not well on the entities level. Then another voice was heard.

"Get out of here, we don't want you here."

At this point Ed crept up behind the medium and withdrew a cross from his pocket. He held it an inch from her neck. The voice cried out, "What are you doing? No, don't do that! Get out! No! Get out!" Then the voice pleaded, "Don't do that! Take it away! Please, take it away!"

Peter's voice could be heard once more. Ed asked him, "Are you there, Peter?"

"Yes, but please help me."

"We are going to help you and Maria. We will find a way."

"Thank you. Hurry, before they come back. I am damned, but I don't want them to hurt anyone else."

"You won't be damned. You must ask God for help first."

"Oh, God help me!"

The entities began attacking Peter again.

"No! Get away! No! I won't do it again."

Ed demanded, "Don't give in to him, Peter."

"I won't give in. They won't get me!"

"I would like Maria to ask you a question. Go ahead, Maria."

"Why did you do this to me when I did you no harm? Why did you make me a prisoner and persecute my family and me? Why did you involve me like this?"

"Because you are an open vessel. You had no protections

about you. You have invited hardship and disaster. If not from me, then from any other entity. I can't explain it to you. You have to understand how open and vulnerable you are."

"Why did you make a prisoner out of me? Make me suffer the way you did? Deny me all of the divine things which God gave me? You took away all of my potentials, even the man I was supposed to marry. You took my good fortune and success away. There is nothing I can do . . . all the doors are locked on me. Why did you do this? Does it make you happy? Is it because of your jealousy? Your vanity? Your egotism? Neither you nor the demons have any divine power over God to take, to isolate, to imprison me and my family, to take all our rights, our talents, our gifts. You destroyed them. Does that make you feel good?"

A spirit guide steps in to speak for Peter.

"May I speak, Maria? I offer this to you for the edification of your soul. That which has been brought before you is truly tormented in spirit. We ask that you grant him your charity. For, indeed, that soul shall suffer far more than from anything that you could inflict upon him. Indeed, it is wrongful for any spirit, just as it is wrongful for any man, to assume control over any other entities which God has created and put on Earth. If we are to be unlike those demonic things which tread the Earth in various forms, we must call upon the bit of good that is in all of us. We ask you, Maria, do something that is, naturally, most difficult for you. Grant him forgiveness."

Maria answered tearfully, "God have mercy on your soul."

Thank you, Maria. We will now take this spirit and we will show him the way that he can make retribution for all the wrong that he has done.

Many humans born on this Earth are subject to being open channels. They cannot control it. Many do not know that they are open channels and cannot understand how they can be under such an affliction. It does not mean that the person who is an open channel and is used by the spirits is necessarily evil in heart. It does not necessarily happen to everyone who does not believe in God or who does not consecrate himself to God. Even those closest to God are very susceptible to being preyed upon. We must constantly keep our guard up. We must always be learning. Maria, do you know how much others shall learn because of your troubles? You must know this; great mercy and blessings will be shed upon you if you can accept the trials that have come to you in this manner. You have brought before the eyes of many, the terrible devastation that is brought upon one by an inhuman source. Only you can decide now whether you will allow this to unsettle you for the rest of your life or you will use it for your enlightenment.

Remember, not all spirits are evil. You are not aware of how many times you have had gifts from good spirits in your life. Because good spirits lead you to do good deeds, for which you can be joyful, you have not acknowledged that the good deeds have come from an outside influence. Those spirits which are demonic and help to destroy your life are often very easy to identify. Good spirits cannot look for recognition because then you would not believe that the things we do are of a good nature. However, because human nature is as weak as it is, it is very much impressed by these fantastic things which you witness.

It is a mixed blessing which comes to you, Maria. In a short time she (the medium) will awaken from her sleep and will discuss various ways for you to set up building blocks around you. You see, you were born with a big chink in your aura; one whole part is missing. Sometimes, when we are born, these things happen. They cannot be blamed upon any particular manifestations. Those things which happen to you in physical life, yes, those are controlled by mortal men. Have greater understanding of what has happened to you from the spirit side. I begin to feel another evil spirit coming.

The voice changed once again from deep and peaceful, to coarse and guttural:

"Despicable! They are vicious and scandalous! If I were you, I would not believe one word. Do you hear? Not one word would I believe from the lips of those people. They are slanderous! I am pure. Do you understand? I can give you everything that you desire. I can give you beauty, all the things that are pleasant, everything that is nice. I wouldn't do anything bad to you. Speak to me!"

Ed Warren answered, "What is your name?"

"I will not answer!"

"Can you describe yourself?"

"I am ugly-looking. I have a horrible face. My eyes are deep sunk. I have gross hair all over my body. I am black all over. My skin is coarse. What else do you want to know?"

"What do you call yourself?"

"I am resentful of this . . . I am resentful of this!"

Once again, Ed crept up behind the medium with a crucifix in his hand and sent the entity into a howling rage of pain, forcing it from the medium.

Since that time, Maria has set up building blocks around herself for protection and has remained free of demonic attacks.

After nearly half a century of continuous torment, Maria has won her war against the negative forces, and Peter has finally been put to rest.

The Ghosts Of West Point

When Ed and Lorraine Warren received a call from the Commanding General of West Point, they were flattered. Imagine their surprise when they were asked to investigate a haunting. West Point, that formidable bastion of logical thinking, the alma mater of Robert E. Lee, Douglas MacArthur and many others. Haunted? The General himself asking to search for a ghost?

Needless to say, they were quick to accept and get involved in one of the most complicated investigations ever.

It was a clear October day and the academy had sent a huge Army limousine to Connecticut for Ed and Lorraine and their entourage for the drive to West Point. Cindy, an investigator who works with Ed and Lorraine, and your author were fortunate to be included in the investigation. After a long ride through the beautiful hills and valleys of New York State, we arrived at the gates of the famous institution. Our adventure began.

After a brief tour of the grounds, we were taken to visit a major who was our contact for this adventure. From his office, we were taken to the site of the haunting, the Colonel Sylvanus Thayer house, which was the Superintendent's quarters.

Deliver Us From Evil

The building was a white-painted brick structure in the
Federal style with two stories, a garret and an iron lace-
work porch all around. It was named after the first officer to
occupy it, the fourth Superintendent of West Point.

On our tour of the house, we were taken to the cellar
where two variations of psychic phenomena continuously
occur. The cellar at one time had housed Colonel Thayer's
office and the downstairs kitchen. It also contained a small
bunkroom where he could sleep nights when he worked
extremely late. This room, which still housed a small bed, was
the scene of a recurrent bit of psychokinesis (the movement
of objects through mind over matter). The neatly made bed
was constantly being unmade by an invisible entity. The bed
would be fixed and a short while later, even though it was
impossible for anyone to have gotten down there, the covers
would again be tossed about. In the downstairs kitchen, there
is a breadboard with a large wet spot in the middle. The spot
never dries. It has remained wet for years and, seemingly,
nothing can be done to dry it.

In many other rooms in the house, apparitions have
been seen flitting about, only to be gone a few seconds later.
Footsteps and knocks on the doors and walls have been
heard. Many times doors have mysteriously opened and
closed by themselves.

Lorraine wandered through the house. She paused to meditate in each room, trying to pick up impressions of ghostly inhabitants, if any. In one of the upstairs rooms she could feel the presence of an elderly, strong-willed woman. In another room she sensed a pleasant, happily married couple.

We examined the upstairs rooms extensively (we were provided a photographer by West Point officials) and proceeded to move downstairs. While walking down the somewhat steep stairs I felt as if I were being pushed, but no one was directly behind me. Now, I was flying through the air in what seemed to be slow motion. I could see the General's aide coming toward me, about to catch me. He too, seemed to be moving in slow motion. I wondered if I could have possibly offended the strong-willed woman whose presence Lorraine felt.

Lorraine and Ed had been asked to lecture at the auditorium that evening. The lecture went well. The subject held the interest of the many cadets and officers who were present. In fact, during the customary question and answer period that followed, we were told about an incident that had been witnessed many times by a number of cadets. A ghost had been seen in one particular room of the dorm by over twenty men including six officers. More about that later.

When the program was over that night we were asked by

two Major's and their wives to hold an séance at the Colonel Sylvanus Thayer house. In retrospect it almost seems unreal. Ed and Lorraine Warren, at conservative old West Point by invitation, seated on the floor, hands joined and forming a circle, two very serious, very logical Army Majors and their wives.

An attempt was made to contact an earthbound spirit during the séance, but none would join our group that night. (An earthbound spirit is a person who, because of great emotional shock at the time of his death, does not pass over correctly and remains attached to this plane.) There were, however, many impressions picked up.

Lorraine saw a man in the uniform of the 1800's, his name began with G, she said it was something like Green or Greer. She told those present that he was very sad . . . that he wanted to be left alone. She said that he definitely had a great guilt feeling, that he was a General's aide and he was black. The Major protested that it couldn't have been. There was never a black aide at the Point at that time. On that note the séance ended.

Approximately a week after our return home, Lorraine received a call from the Commanding General of West Point. He said that he had personally researched the history of West Point and had found that, indeed, there had been a black man named Greer who was an aide during the 1800's. He went on to say that Greer was arrested for murdering a man on the grounds of the academy. He was later granted clemency. Greer is not at rest.

The next day an officer from West Point called and told Lorraine that each night since their visit a ghost had appeared in a room of one of the dorms. It was the same ghost that had been seen by the officers and cadets many times before the Warren's visit. The entity's frequency has increased lately because of the greater recognition it has been getting. This is a natural phenomenon among ghost hunters.

The ghost wore a nineteenth century uniform and carried a rifle. He walked through a wall into the center of the room and then exited again by walking through another wall. The wall through which he entered was always quite hot from the radiator which was against it. Whenever the entity came through, the radiator turned icy cold. Could this entity be in any way connected with Greer? Could this be Greer's victim?

We had been bound to strict secrecy by officials of West Point to protect it from possible ridicule. An unknown cadet (West Point assumes) decided that he was not a part of that agreement. Within a few days, every major newspaper, radio station and television network was talking about the West Point Ghost and our investigation. We were told by the Army that any further investigation by us was out of the question until the culprit who had called the press was found.

A young midshipman from Annapolis, anxious to grab some publicity and at the same time cause grief for West Point claimed that the whole ghost story was a hoax which he had created. He said that he had climbed onto the roof of the dorm and lowered himself over the side just above the second floor windows. There, with a flashlight and a foggy slide, he projected the image into the room, thereby creating the ghost. He said that he had done this for a full week, beginning Halloween night. West Point was quick to point out, however, some discrepancies in his story.

They pointed out that the haunting took place on the first, not the second floor. Over twenty people witnessed the apparition. They saw it very clearly walk through the wall and into the center of the room. The radiator had turned cold as the entity appeared. Finally they noted that the haunting had been seen each night for a full week before Halloween.

When we asked officials of West Point for permission to use photographs made for us by the photographer that they provided, they emphatically said, "NO!" The day after we made the request the F.B.I. paid us a visit. We were told that we could keep the photographs provided that we never use them in public. We were asked to sign a contract that provided penalties for violation.

We hope someday we will be allowed by West Point officials to conclude our investigation. Until then, some of the dormitory rooms will continue to be sealed off, a mystery will remain unsolved and a ghost will continue its nightly walks in the halls of West Point.

Deliver Us From Evil

Where evil lurks and worshippers of its madness dwell, the beauty of nature becomes a grotesque parody. So it is in one particular valley in New England. There, the ancient road narrowly winds between twisted, stunted trees which claw the air above ominously. Low ledges of lichen-covered rocks jut out occasionally and crevices seep water that undermines the lane. The few dark houses which exist in that area seldom appear to see the light of day. Even the sun seems to shun those malignant woods. At the bottom of the valley, extending for acres in great desolation, is an abandoned sand pit with huge mounds of earth erupting out of a plain of ponds and puddles, foul marshes and insanely misshapen oaks. There lies hidden the very heart of the evil.

The cold light of the full moon creates weird shadows around the great dunes in the sand pit. Behind one of those mounds, flickering candlelight plays over the black-clad coven, while at the altar (a stolen gravestone) the high priestess drinks blood from a chalice. The coven chants, spellbound, as their mistress raises her dagger over the struggling rooster. The chanting drones on, getting louder until it reaches a peak and the priestess shrieks, "Hail, Satan!" Then she drives her knife down forcefully into the helpless, screaming bird. The silence in that valley of shadows is shattered by the echoes of the tragedy carried on the murmuring winds.

Laura was only eighteen years old, yet she was on the brink of destruction when she first sought help from Ed and Lorraine in 1971. Pathetically desperate, she related her bizarre story to them. A year later she visited them again, begging for help, but unable to accept it, for by then she was already in the grasp of the evil upon which she had called.

Laura had always been attracted to the occult, particularly the dark side. In April 1971, she believed that if she really tried, she could "conjure" something up. Her boyfriend had just told her that he no longer wanted to see her. Perhaps the spirit world could help. She called upon Satan, but nothing happened. Disappointed, she decided to go to bed. When she walked over to her mirror she saw, in the depths of it, a mist forming. It seemed to be taking on the features of a hairy, partially decayed being, half human, half wolf! It had large, penetrating, luminous eyes that fixed her horrified gaze to them. It was impossible to turn away. After she stared at it for what seemed like an eternity, the face turned white as if it were a negative. Then it faded away and as it released Laura from its stare, she could feel a shocking change of mood. She felt that she could actually kill someone. She also felt morbidly attracted to that face and she wanted to see it once more. Once again Laura tried to summon the creature, but to no avail.

As the days passed Laura began to believe that her boyfriend's best friend, Donald, had caused their separation. An intense hatred of Donald grew inside Laura. In fact, the hatred became so intense that she decided to kill him. She warned Donald of the consequences if he continued to interfere. He would not listen.

The wolf demon appeared again in Laura's mirror and she asked it to help her. Under its guidance, she began to work on an obscure voodoo rite.

With a pail of water in front of her, Laura concentrated on making Donald's face appear on the surface of the water. When she saw his face clearly, she stabbed it again and again with a large kitchen knife. The demon had told her that if she concentrated hard enough, the water would turn to blood and Donald would die. It didn't work.

Laura knew that Black Magic, if performed properly, would work. She decided to try again, this time intent on killing herself after she did away with Donald. Immediately after that decision, the wolf-demon appeared and demanded that she forget both her boyfriend and Donald . . . there were better things for her to do in the service of her new found lord, Satan. She took the advice and eventually did forget them. She redirected her love in a new, unfortunate direction.

It is interesting to note here that during Laura's first interview with Ed and Lorraine, as she told them of the wolf-demon, Ed began coughing. A strange, sulfuric odor filled the room and irritated his lungs. Laura was obsessed and the entity which attacked her made its presence known to Ed.

For the next few weeks Laura glorified in the feeling of power which she had gained and, searching for more, she asked for additional demons to enter her body.

Near midnight on the second day of a vacation on Cape Cod, Laura felt a strong urge to leave her friend's house and go for a walk. With a blanket wrapped around her for a cape, she made her way through the dark, narrow, winding streets until she arrived at an ancient cemetery. There, she threaded her way around the worn stones. She enjoyed herself immensely, Laura felt quite at home. She came back out through the old wooden gate and sat down on the stonewall that bordered the old burial place. Soon, a young man about twenty years old, who was slightly drunk, came wandering by. He saw Laura sitting there and asked if he could join her. She neither encouraged him nor discouraged him so he sat down and engaged her in small talk. Slowly, without saying a word, Laura wrapped her arms around his neck and drew him closer. He stopped talking and, pleased with his success, moved closer to her, closed his eyes and prepared for the coming kiss. It never came. Instead, Laura suddenly jerked him to her and, baring her teeth, she sunk them deeply into his throat and drank the blood that spurted out. The young man suddenly became sober. He managed to break away from her and, pressing his hand to his neck to stop the flow of blood, he ran off into the night. He glanced back over his shoulder once as if he expected all the spirits of Hell to be after him.

Laura didn't know what had come over her. She was ashamed of what she had done and began to think that she really was insane.

Laura became the high priestess of a satanic coven which held its rituals in the deserted sand pits at the bottom of the valley. While they were practicing their ceremonies one moonlit night they were discovered by the police.

Laura had just finished the invocation to Satan and, as the others watched, she made ready to slit the throat of the rooster in order to drain its blood into the chalice. As she raised the dagger, two blinding shafts of light focused on her and three policemen jumped out of the car. Two of them stood guard, making sure no one escaped. The third rushed to the altar in an attempt to find out what Laura was doing.

By the time the officer got to Laura's side, she had hidden the knife. When he asked why the rooster was there, she told him that it was their pet. He was not fully convinced but he had no knowledge of witchcraft, so that thought didn't enter his mind. Since there was no evidence of a violation of the law, the police left.

Laura developed an incredible lust for blood. It was so intense that at times she couldn't avoid the strong urge and found herself doing whatever she could to satisfy it, including drinking her own blood!

Laura wasn't alone in that inhuman lust. Kathy, a close friend whom she had introduced to black magic, also shared the ghoulish desire. Many times when they were unable to find a rooster or other appropriate sacrifice, they would draw blood from their own arms with a hypodermic needle and then, mixing it with wine, would indulge their craving. Eventually this practice caused Laura to be hospitalized with an infected arm. Doctors even considered amputation. Until that time she had no qualms about slicing her arm in any manner necessary to draw out more and more blood.

At this point in the second interview with Ed Warren, when she discussed her hospitalization, Ed produced a cup of liquid that looked remarkably like blood. He handed it to Laura and asked her to drink it. She became suspicious at first, thinking it might be medicine. When she realized that it wasn't, she drank the liquid. This proved to Ed that she

134   www.edandlorrainewarren.com

would drink blood without a moment's hesitation. After she drank it, she said that it could not have been blood because it didn't taste like it.

Soon Laura became fascinated with cemeteries and the dead. She spent practically every night wandering around the old graveyards in her area. She and Kathy made plans to dig up a body but at the last minute decided against it.

Laura's thirst for blood increased. She allowed herself to be picked up by young men who were looking for sex. She directed them to the sand pit area and when they became involved in a heated embrace, she sunk her teeth in their necks, drinking their blood.

More black masses were performed in honor of Satan. Both Laura and Kathy stole religious articles from local churches. They burned Bibles and contaminated holy water. At every opportunity they defiled the word of God.

Laura could no longer understand what was happening to her. She felt great happiness and power while performing her ugly deeds, but afterwards she felt guilty and ashamed. She began to believe that she was going insane, but she couldn't stop herself. The entity that she had called had actually taken control of her life. She began to see the face of the wolf-demon in strangers on the street. Even when she looked at her friend Kathy she was horrified to see that face. Laura was beyond the point of return.

Candlemass, a Christian holy day, was coming and Laura and Kathy made plans to defile it. They would hold a mass and offer a human sacrifice this time to the devil. Kathy asked Laura to open her arm once more so that they could use her blood but it was badly abscessed again and Laura turned her down. They would have to look elsewhere.

At first they thought that they should kidnap a baby for the sacrifice but Kathy came up with a more evil plan.

Kathy hated her father. She knew that if she used him as their sacrifice, Satan would be satisfied. She described her gruesome plan to Laura in detail. She would stab him and then tear his body apart and gorge herself on his flesh. Kathy's eyes gleamed madly in her possessed state, her face contorted with the satanic laughter of the demonic entities which were taking complete control of her.

Laura fled the apartment half crazed with fear. She had never seen Kathy in such a state. She swore to herself that she would never see Kathy again and promised not to perform the profane rites which had become so much a part of her life. Within a week the two were together once more, their voices echoing in obscene worship from behind a mound in the sand pits.

A cacophony of violins, tambourines, flutes and drums

created the absurd accompaniment to the lewd dancing at the devil's mass. The participants drank from a jug of wine mixed with wormwood, absinthe, morning glory seeds, nightshade, devil's nettle, laurel leaves and blood . . . a horribly potent witch's brew.

The full moon glistened on the naked bodies as they ran faster and faster in an ever-expanding circle until, finally, they collapsed in a heap, too exhausted to move. Laura lay there panting heavily. Her ecstasy of the moment blanked out her memory of the letter that she had mailed that afternoon during a fit of desperation. It read:

"Help me please! I'm into black magic too deeply now and I'm afraid that I'll never get out. We're going too far . . . our Lord wants us to give him humans now, no more animals. I don't want to, but I can't turn back! It seems to be my whole life. I saw the wolf in the mirror again. He said that I would live only a little while longer. What can I do? I don't want to die! Help me!"

The coven continues with their grisly rites. They worship the evil which they called upon, never will they control it for they are no longer in control of themselves. In each, in the hidden recesses of their mind, a subconscious voice rebels and, unheard, screams in agony, "Someone, please someone, deliver us from this evil!"

The Case Of Douglas Dean

by Betty Joan Burr

The secret church files of the case on which "The Exorcist" is based are open to very few people. One of those allowed to see them is Ed Warren, a demonologist, who is considered a leading expert on ghosts and spirits and who has investigated a number of alleged possessions. Warren has read the testimony by the many doctors and priests who were part of the "Exorcist" case.

To get a report of what those confidential files contain, I went to Ed Warren's home one warm, moonless night last summer. The house was shrouded by heat mists sifting down from the Connecticut hills. It seemed isolated, solitary. Inside the air was cool, almost chilly, despite the summer heat. The soft fire-red glow of living room lights crept across crevices in dark wood walls. A strange mood - some warning vibrations - hit me but I shook it off as an overactive imagination.

"You are being subjected to very bad vibrations in this house," Warren warned me at the door, "because below this level is a ceremonial room where magic is performed and where my collection of satanic articles is kept. Their vibrations affect this whole house."

With that cheerful introduction Warren ushered me into

a chair, assuring me that I was in no danger if I would follow his instructions. I promised, crossed my fingers, turned on the tape recorder, and asked him about demons.

"There is not one iota of doubt in my mind that devils and demons exist," Warren began. "They walk the earth only through possession of the physical body of a human being, when a person no longer has power over his body - the enemy just takes over. Spirits also appear through oppression, by telling a person what to do. Oppression occurs the moment someone gets the idea to delve into any kind of supernatural activity - using an Ouija board, holding séances, or practicing ESP. These activities are invitations to malign spirits, and to eventual possession by those spirits.

"I want you to understand, by the way," Warren said to me, "that because you are writing about this, you are already under oppression."

The words set the ends of my hair tingling. Bits of perspiration broke out on my back. For a moment, I considered dropping the whole subject. But if I went back without a story, I'd have a hard time explaining why. The choice was simple, demons or unemployment.

So I sat on the edge of my chair, kept my skepticism handy, and asked Warren to tell me about the case on which the story of "The Exorcist" is based, the possession of a boy to whom the Church has given the fictitious name of Douglas Dean. Warren's account is based upon his reading of Church records and is repeated here just as he told it to me.

The terror began for Douglas Dean on January 15, 1949, in Mount Rainier, Maryland. He was 14 when possession began. The demons were invited in, we think, by his parents and aunt. They had used an Ouija board to contact the spirit world.

The first indications were scratching sounds in the house in floorboards, ceilings, and walls. The family blamed mice and called in exterminators, which of course did no good.

Then the boy began levitating. Sitting quietly in a chair, he would suddenly be transported across the room. He'd lie in a bed that would then lift slowly into the air. Bed sheets rose as if they had been heavily starched.

At first, everyone thought the incidents were funny. But suddenly Douglas started yelling in foreign languages and screaming obscenities at his family.

At that point the thoroughly frightened parents called in their Lutheran minister. He suggested that Douglas be taken to Georgetown University, a Catholic school in Washington, D.C., run by Jesuit priests who had studied cases of diabolical possession. That advice was the first warning to the family that something supernatural had happened.

At Georgetown, Douglas was placed under observation in the university hospital. Priests wanted to see if there were physical causes for the boy's actions. Numerous doctors went over every inch of his body. Psychiatrists tried to talk to him. None of the doctors could find any medical reason for the weird occurrences. Testimony from these experts is in the Church files as part of the evidence that possession did take place.

The symptoms became increasingly worse. Douglas described details of historical events he couldn't possibly have experienced. He also showed precognition by talking about events in the future.

He described places the demons took him, giving accurate details to prove he had been there. I can't tell you where they were or describe them, because if you knew, the demons could get you. Priests at Georgetown concluded that the astral, or spiritual body of the child had been taken elsewhere by the demons, since his physical body stayed in the room at all times.

Douglas continued talking in foreign languages to priests who questioned him in French, Latin, and Italian. Sometimes he even corrected their pronunciation.

He could levitate objects into the air and move them around. Once, when his mother called a priest at Georgetown, the possessed boy made the phone table explode in front of her through a process in which a high-pitched, inaudible sound makes things shatter.

Different voices came from the boy - a shrill falsetto; a low guttural grunt; and animal groans, clucking and chirping. He screamed and screeched for hours.

His physical body went through excruciating contortions - the arms would go up straight in back of him and his legs twisted around the trunk of his body - something no human being could do in a conscious state.

Nauseating smells and large heaps of excrement came from his body, although the boy had eaten almost nothing. He would vomit 20 or 30 times a day - huge piles of vomit, some of it looking like hair. Obviously, the physical body wasn't producing these wastes. They were brought in by the demons through teleportation - the power of mind used to transport substances by breaking them down into their tiniest parts.

Many times people in the room heard a slap, and a red mark appeared on the boy's face. His body bloated until it seemed ready to explode. The face twisted into terrible contorted shapes, his lips and head puffed up like a balloon filled with water, and his eyes bulged out as if he were choking.

Despite his weakened condition, Douglas showed

tremendous strength, and as many as ten of the investigating priests were needed to hold him down on the floor. If he got free, he would rise to the ceiling and clutch at it with his hands and feet, a diabolical look on his face.

Satisfied that no medical or psychological reasons could explain the condition of the boy, the priests recommended exorcism.

The family decided to put Douglas in the home of an aunt in St. Louis where the rites could be performed. But she couldn't stand having him there, and all hospitals refused to take him.

Finally, the boy was placed in a monastery near St. Louis where the rites of exorcism were begun. Douglas had been baptized into the Catholic Church at Georgetown, but before the exorcism could proceed, he had to take Communion. For four hours priests struggled to get the Communion Host into the boy's mouth, but his jaws were clenched tight by the demons. Finally, they succeeded in forcing the Host past his gritted teeth.

The priest who was assigned to perform the exorcism was a man in his early 50's. He began a fast to purify himself, losing 50 pounds in all, and stayed constantly at the boy's bedside as he prepared himself for the struggle to come.

Then it began. While several other priests held the boy

down, the exorcist recited a litany. He held a large towel in front of him. Even so, phlegm would come from the boy's mouth, half a pint at a time, and fire across the room, go over the towel and hit the exorcist in the eyes.

The exorcism consisted of ritual and prayers recited by the priest. But the boy had to say "I renounce Satan and all of his works," and two other ritual words in order to end the possession. The words wouldn't come from his mouth.

It was also necessary that the demons give the time of their departure from the physical body. When a demon is commanded in the name of Jesus Christ to reveal his name, he must. But these demons refused to do so until the boy said two words. The case looked hopeless.

The struggle went on through Easter Sunday 1949. On Easter the demons erupted in some of the most violent manifestations of the whole case screaming, spitting, yelling curses. But these terrors must have been their death battle - the next day the boy was finally able to speak the ritual words and was freed of possession. When he spoke, bright red welts popped out on his chest, spelling out the names of the demons and the time of their exorcism. Priests discovered that three separate demons had invaded this human being. The two-and-a-half month terror was over.

That was the end of Warren's story. He told me that

The Case Of Douglas Dean

"Douglas Dean", now 38 years old is living a normal life. Dean's recollections are part of the Church records. In Ed Warren's view, this testimony and evidence in the files from doctors, priests, and other reliable witnesses are proof that Douglas Dean was possessed by diabolical spirits.

I thanked Ed Warren for his help, unplugged my tape recorder, and left the house with great relief.

The darkness of the night was deeper than ever, throwing a shadow over my car. Suddenly I remembered Warren's warning, "You are already oppressed." Before I started the car, I took the precautions he advised. "Imagine a Christ light around you, a white glow enveloping you, your car, and your house. If you think anything evil is nearby say "In the name of Jesus Christ, I command you to go back where you came from." Then cross yourself.

Maybe it was silly. But I felt a lot better after taking Warren's advice.

Glossary

Apparition: An unusual or unexpected sight. A ghostly figure.

Automatic Writing: Writing executed without the agent's volition and sometimes without his knowledge.

Circumambulism: The formation of a circle on foot in a ritualistic manner.

Clairvoyant: One who has the power to detect objects not present to the senses.

Demon: Evil spirit

Demonology: The study of evil spirits.

Entity: An independent, separate or self-contained existence.

Exorcism: The practice of freeing evil spirits.

Infestation: Living in or on as a parasite.

Macabre: Having death as a subject.

Malevolent: Having, showing or arising from intense, often vicious ill will, spite or hatred.

Medium: An individual held to be a channel of communication between the earthly world and the world of spirits.

Occult: Relating to supernatural agencies, their effects and knowledge of them.

Glossary

Ouija: A board used with a planchette to seek spiritualistic or telepathic messages.

Possession: A psychological state in which an individual's normal personality is replaced by another.

Precognition: Clairvoyance relating to an event or state not yet experienced.

Psychometry: Divination of facts concerning an object or its owner through contact with or proximity to the object.

Psychokenesis: Movement of objects through mind over matter.

Satanism: Innate wickedness. Obsession with or an affinity for evil.

Supernatural: Of or relating to an order of existence beyond the visible observable universe.

Telepathically: Communication from one mind to another through mental channels.

Voodooism: A religion derived from African ancestor worship. The practice of witchcraft.

About Ed and Lorraine Warren

Ed and Lorraine Warren are often called America's original ghost hunters. The Warrens were married at the age of 18 and since then have traveled throughout the United States, Canada, Mexico, Australia, Scotland, Great Britain and Europe and many more places investigating thousands of reports of haunted houses, demons, vampires, werewolves and cases of black witchcraft. They consulted with police departments, clergy of all faiths, hospitals and psychiatrists.

At age five, Ed Warren (September 7, 1926 - August 23, 2006) lived in a house that was haunted by a former tenant. Ed devoted his life to the study of the supernatural. Before his death, he was recognized in the world of the occult as a leading demonologist.

Lorraine Warren, a mediumistic, has been clairvoyant (a person with the ability to see things not in sight) since she was a child. Lorraine believes it is a gift that has progressed. She points out that upon going into a home on an initial investigation or for an séance, she is able to tell if there is something of a paranormal nature going on.

Everywhere they speak, Ed and Lorraine Warren captivate their audience. They have lectured in many of the nation's leading colleges, cruise ships, social clubs, local events and many large lecture halls. Their provocative lectures and stimulating question and answer periods leave audiences of every age and sex literally spellbound. Besides speaking the Warrens did radio, television specials, documentaries and hosted a Cable TV Show, "Seekers of the Supernatural". Ed and Lorraine were both professional artists.

Lorraine Warren can currently be seen on two TV Series; "A Haunting", which airs on the Discovery Channel and Discovery Science channel and "Paranormal State" which is described as a docu-drama reality television series which airs on the A&E Channel.

Additional cases by the Warren's can be found at their website, www.edandlorrainewarren.com.

About The Author J. F. Sawyer

J. F. Sawyer is an actor, director, psychic investigator and lecturer as well as an author. He is a veteran of numerous radio and television talk show and many many lectures done throughout New England on the subject of psychic phenomena. He has spent quite a few years researching the subject and has assisted Ed and Lorraine Warren in many of their investigations. When not out addressing the public or hunting ghosts, he spends most of his time at home in Fairfield, Connecticut.

For More information about Ed and Lorraine Warren,
please check out the following:

www.edandlorrainewarren.com
www.seekersofthesupernatural.com
www.facebook.com/edandlorrainewarren
www.myspace.com/edandlorrainewarren
www.youtube.com/edandlorrainewarren
www.twitter.com/1stghosthunters

Deliver Us From Evil

www.edandlorrainewarren.com

Lightning Source UK Ltd.
Milton Keynes UK
UKHW022230130421
381939UK00009B/2355